See You Soon

NC Marshall

Prologue

I know you are there before I even turn around. There's a shift in the air, the wind changes its direction ever so slightly, but just enough to make me aware you're behind me. I don't dare turn to look at you. I want to pretend that I'm imagining it, but the busy street is full of people and I don't want to make any more commotion than is necessary.

I calmly place my shopping bags on the pavement, trying my best to avoid the stares from passersby who have noticed that something isn't quite right. I look down at the beautifully wrapped parcel that sits on the ground, its paper packaging now soaking up the rain from the damp pavement. In it is a necklace, a birthday present. I was looking forward to seeing her face when she opened it. That's not going to happen now.

A little girl of about seven years old clutching a large, brown fuzzy teddy bear comes out of the store next to me. Her tightly curled hair is pulled into pigtails secured with bright pink grips. She smiles sweetly, then looks puzzled as her mother mutters something, then drags her quickly away.

I still have my back to you, but I can now see a reflection in the shop window that I am standing near. The image is blurred in the rain-streaked glass. I watch silently as you take a step closer to me and raise an item from inside your jacket pocket, the hazy sun shines against it and I realise it's a small handgun. Although I'm shocked, I knew there was a possibility that this day was going to come.

Now panic sets in around us.

"It's a gun," I hear a man shout from somewhere close.

"Someone call the police," another yells loudly.

People start to run. The sound of screaming rings loudly in my ears. The busy street quickly clears, now becoming too quiet and extremely eerie for a Saturday afternoon in a normally busy city centre.

"How did you find me?" I ask, still with my back to you. My voice shakes, as does my whole body.

You don't answer.

I close my eyes. Tears start to stream down my cheeks, fear raging inside of me, or is it fury? I can hear sirens in the distance. Their noise gets gradually louder. Help is on its way, but it's too late now, you have hold of me around the neck. I don't attempt to get free. I'm too traumatised. Too frightened. My knees give way, but your hold prevents me from falling to the ground.

Your grip is so tight I can't breathe. With one hand you grab hold of my hair, wrenching my head painfully to one side. *1,2,3 wake up, 1,2,3 wake up!*

But this isn't another dream. The silent and desperate plea to my subconscious won't work this time.

I scream out as you put the gun to my temple. The cold hard metal penetrates through my skull. Your breath is heavy and hot on my ear. Your breathing is fast, but still you don't speak.

I close my eyes, squeezing them shut as tightly as I can, waiting for the trigger to be pulled. The bullet. My death. But it doesn't come as quickly as I thought it would.

Police sirens grow louder and blue lights now blaze behind my eyes as I wait for the sound that is going to be the last thing I ever hear. There is no bright light for me to enter. There are no angels or lost loved ones waiting—maybe they will come later. I don't see all the significant times of my life; specific memories, important life milestones or the people in my life that I hold dearest. Instead, my mind is clear and calm. I'm not afraid anymore. I'm ready.

Then suddenly, I hear it, the deafening bang. A noise that vaguely sounds like my own voice crying out echoes in my ears as I fall towards the damp pavement. The police sirens sound fades away. The light behind my eyes weakens as I continue to fall. Then I see nothing but darkness.

I don't feel myself hit the ground.

Part One

Chapter 1

The e-mail was the catalyst that started everything. A long chain of events that I never saw coming and would succeed to turn my life on its axis. I could have never predicted what was about to happen. How could I?

It was early evening ending an early summer's day. I had recently finished work at a city centre restaurant and was on my way home after enduring a busy nine-hour shift that had been full of customers who seemed to want to do nothing more than look down their snooty noses at me. My feet were aching and the smell of hot food that clung to my uniform was beginning to make me feel queasy. The bus home was running late, nothing out of the ordinary on my frequent short commute that had become a regular part of my unglamorous daily routine. I waited at the bus stop playing with my mobile phone to pass the time, eager to get home and slip my aching limbs into a hot bubble bath.

The e-mail blinked up onto the screen as I trawled through the numerous items of junk mail, erasing ruthlessly. I was just about to delete it along with all the others, but the name of the sender registered instantly and a part of my past came rushing back to me along with it. Alison Martin. She had sent the message to an e-mail account I rarely used anymore. I couldn't believe that after almost sixteen years she hadn't changed her e-mail address and still had mine. I was surprised she even remembered me at all after the amount of time that had passed.

The message had been sent three days ago. I felt a brief smile flick across my lips as I rushed to open the message from my old childhood friend. Memories flashed through my mind, her face as clear as day, although I had no idea what she looked like in the present. We hadn't parted on bad terms, but then they hadn't necessarily been particularly that good either. Still, I found myself eager to hear what she had to say. I began to read as the bus home approached the stop and the long queue finally started to move. I scanned the first few lines of the neatly typed words, causing the smile on my face to quickly vanish. The weight on my legs seemed suddenly heavier. I missed my footing and half-fell onto the elderly man standing in front of me in the queue that had now come to a halt.

"Are you alright, love?" asked the man, as he kindly helped me up to my feet.

I managed a feeble nod in his direction. He nodded back politely as he moved away and continued towards the bus. I buried the phone in my cardigan pocket and followed him. Settling down at a window seat near the back of the bus, I reopened the message. I didn't want to read it; I wanted to pretend that I hadn't even received it, but I knew I couldn't do that. I read the message three times before it finally sank in:

Hi Emily,

How are you? I hope you are well. Forgive me for contacting you after all of these years, out of the blue in this way. I know that we haven't spoken for so long, but I need to let someone know, and you see, you were the first person that came to mind. I no longer have a contact number for you so I couldn't call. I'm relying on the fact you are still using the same e-mail address as you had back in school to get this. Basically Em, I'm in trouble. Big, big trouble. I'm scared and I really need someone to talk to. I don't know what to do. Please give me a call as soon as you get this. I've attached my telephone number below.

Speak soon, I hope,
Ali x

I quickly dialled the number at the bottom of the e-mail, not really thinking through what I was going to say. I hadn't seen or spoken to Ali in over fifteen years. I wasn't too sure why after so long she would choose me to contact in such an emergency—and it seemed like an emergency—judging by the words she had used in her message, albeit vague. It didn't matter. I needed to speak to her. The phone rang and went straight through to her machine, so I left her a message with my phone number and told her to call me straight back, when she had the chance. She didn't.

A few days later and I still had no word from Ali. I'd called and e-mailed her back, but she didn't answer or reply to any of my attempts. I fooled myself into thinking that maybe her dilemma had been sorted, that whatever trouble she had referred to in her message had been resolved and she didn't need to speak to me anymore, but I knew that was a long shot. She would have at least called me to tell me she was safe. I knew that even though we were no longer well acquainted, she would have the decency to at least do that.

A few more days passed. I tried to get on with my daily routine and put the e-mail to the back of my mind, but my thoughts kept straying back to Ali and I had a creeping sense of unease that wouldn't leave me. I couldn't describe it, but it was a nagging feeling of dread that just wouldn't go away. A feeling something had happened to her. Something bad. So, I finally decided to take action. Even if was to just put my mind at rest that Ali was safe, I wouldn't settle until I knew for sure.

I dialed the number of the police station into my phone, then sat fidgeting nervously with the edge of the small wooden table in the kitchen of my home.

"Good afternoon, Sandbroke Police Station, Rachael speaking, how can I help?" asked a girl cheerily greeting me on the other side of the line.

"Hi, could I talk to someone regarding an old friend of mine?" Even hearing the name of my old home town made my stomach flip.

"Can I ask what it's regarding?" asked Rachael.

"I think an old friend of mine could be in some sort of trouble. She contacted me recently to tell me that she needed to speak to me. She needed my help," I said hastily, my words rushing out far too fast for such a delicate matter.

"Yes, of course," replied the receptionist unsurpassed. "I'll put you through to one of our officers. Please hold."

Classical music played quietly as I waited for another voice to come on the line.

"Hello, this is Inspector Mayland, how can I help?" a female officer asked.

"Oh, hello," I said, unsure now of what to say. "I just wanted to let you know about a message I received a few days ago. It's from an old friend of mine. It sounds as though she is in some sort of trouble. I just want to check that nothing has been reported." I paused to compose myself. "I'm a little concerned about her."

"Okay, can I take your name?" asked the officer in a soothing tone of voice. I must have sounded as distraught as I felt. I heard her rustling around for a pen.

"Emily, Emily Moore," I replied quickly, my voice shaking.

Inspector Mayland proceeded to take more details from me. "And you say your friend is a local resident here at Sandbroke?"

I paused, feeling foolish. Ali could have moved away from Sandbroke at any time during the fifteen years since I'd last spoken to her. But then, I knew how much she loved the place. I very much doubt she would be far from the area, cutting all ties to it completely.

"Um, I'm not too sure. To be honest it's been a very long time since I had any contact with her."

"But you have reason to believe she could have come to harm?"

"Yes, possibly. I received an e-mail from her saying she needed my help. She sounded quite desperate."

"An e-mail?" The officer sounded skeptical and I instantly regretted making the call. "Okay, what did you say her full name was?"

"I didn't. It's Alison. Alison Martin."

"Oh, I see. Can you hold please, Miss Moore?"

"Yes, that's fine."

Growing more anxious, I heard a click and once again, I was put on hold. It felt like forever before the officer got back to me.

"Miss Moore. I'm sorry to keep you waiting; I just had to check something with my colleague. We are in fact working on a case of a missing person and I can confirm the woman's name is Miss Alison Martin." My heart rate accelerated. I felt as though I was going to pass out. *She was missing.*

"What, when, where?" I stammered, breathlessly.

"She lives over in Cranley Quays now. She was reported missing by a neighbour eight days ago. The police are currently looking into her disappearance. There's been no evidence of any harm to her. Her risk grading has been set as low, meaning we don't believe she is in any immediate danger. Our team is looking into her case now. That's all I can tell you at this point, Miss Moore."

I stayed silent.

"Miss Moore, we are going to have to see that e-mail and you also if possible. Do you live in the area?"

"No. Not anymore," I whispered. The kitchen started to swim around me, forcing me to grip the edge of the table.

"Could you forward us the e-mail please? We will also need to talk to you further as soon as possible. Up to now you are the only person that we know of who had any contact with Miss Martin in the days leading up to her disappearance. It would be good to discuss this face to face if possible."

I swallowed back the lump that had lodged itself squarely in the centre of my throat.

"Or we can sort it out another way. If it's going to be trouble for you," said Inspector Mayland when I didn't immediately respond.

Tears filled my eyes. I knew what I had to do.

"Don't worry," I replied quietly. "I'll come to you. I'll come back to Sandbroke."

Chapter 2

So now, here I am—on a train heading back to the seaside town that I had been born and grown up in. I wish I could say that I am looking forward to going back there after so long. I wish I could say I was going for a holiday, to have a long overdue reunion, to see some familiar faces and relive a perfect youth, but then I would be lying. Sandbroke holds many memories for me that I would much rather forget.

A loud clatter interrupts my thoughts as a train hostess crashes the refreshments trolley straight into the side of my seat, narrowly missing my legs and causing me to jump.

"Oh, I am sorry," she says, flustered. "It's my first day on the job. I haven't learnt how to control this thing yet." Embarrassed, she bends to chase the miniature cans of coke now rolling along the aisle of the crammed carriage.

"Don't worry about it." I force a smile in her direction, my nerves still on edge. The lady sitting next to me gives a wry smile before returning to her book. She has been heavily absorbed in its pages since she joined the train a few hours back.

"Can I get you anything?" the girl asks, pulling at her blazer hem. Composing herself, she gestures to the stack of sandwiches, sweets, and biscuits loaded onto the trolley top. Her cheeks are a bright shade of pink.

"I'll just have a coffee," I say, hoping that a quick intake of caffeine will ease my jitteriness. Though somehow, I doubt it.

My phone starts to ring as I hand the girl some money for my drink and accept the flimsy plastic cup from her accompanied by small pots of UHT milk and far too many sachets of white sugar. I quickly finish the transaction and reach in my handbag to answer the call.

"Hi, darling," I say quietly, as my daughter's voice greets me on the other side of the line.

"Hi, Mum, how's the journey going?"

"Slowly," I reply honestly, stretching my legs out as far as the small space will allow and silently wishing I was back at home with her, back in familiar surroundings. Safe.

"What time are you due to get in?"

I look at my watch. "Another hour and a half or so to go."

"Yuck, rather you than me."

"How did the exam go at school today?" I ask, suddenly remembering that Lucy had an exam earlier this morning.

"Good, I think, but maths has never been my strong point. It was the one I was dreading and I'm just glad it's over to be honest."

"Well, I think you get that from me. I can barely function without a calculator close at hand." The woman next to me glances up from her book and gives a polite smile as if to silently declare that she suffers from the same problem. I take a sip from the hot coffee. It tastes too sweet and far too watery. My stomach churns.

"What's your next exam?"

"English Lit, tomorrow afternoon, last one, then I'm free!"

I laugh at my daughter's excitement at the prospect of finally leaving secondary school behind. Which I'm sure will diminish when she realises how much harder life is once you leave education and enter the real world. I know she will do well in the exams. One area of my life that I have no worries is my daughter's studies; she has always been a bright and studious girl, from being young.

"Are you at Grandma and Grandpa's now?" I ask.

"Yeah, Grandpa met me outside the school after the exam finished. He refused to let me walk back to their house on my own. It's only a ten-minute walk. You would think I was still a kid!"

"In their eyes you are."

"I'm nearly sixteen, Mum."

"I know, I know." I smile at my daughter's purposeful attempt at grown-up tone, which nudges at my heart strings.

"She *is* still a kid!" I hear my dad shout from somewhere in the room near Lucy and I chuckle at his comment. No matter how old she gets, Lucy will always be a little girl in her grandparents' eyes. Mine too, I suppose.

"I was just calling to see how the journey was going Mum, say hi to Auntie Trisha for me when you get to Scotland."

I wince. I'd told Lucy I'm travelling to Glasgow to visit my sister for a couple of days. Only Trisha and my parents know the truth of where I am actually going. Lucy doesn't need to know. I feel sick to the core for lying to her.

"Okay, Lucy, I'll call you tonight. Tell Grandma and Grandpa I'll speak to them later too."

"Great, Mum, will do, speak soon."

I end the call to my daughter. Tears form in my eyes as I look out of the window at the passing landscape, slowly changing as the miles roll on. Beyond the hills, the sea soon starts to creep into view sparkling under the sun. A perfect golden coastline fully emerges a little later, but the wonderful view does nothing to ease the feeling of dread I have in the pit of my stomach. If it wasn't for the memories of this place it would be truly beautiful. I lean back and try to relax, but memories of Ali race through my mind.

*

Ali was one of my best friends from when we were eight years old and in our fourth year of primary school along with Jenna, who we had befriended a year later when she moved to Sandbroke.

Ali and I were inseparable from the start, even though she was a lot more dramatic and showy that I ever was; we had a lot in common and we got on really well. When Jenna joined us the bond was strengthened even more. They are the only true friends I have had. I have a few friends now, but none of them have even come close to the relationship I had with Ali.

Our friendship remained strong all the way through secondary school. I always felt blessed to have friends like Ali and Jenna. We were tightly knit and I felt I could turn to Ali in particular for anything. She was there for me whenever I needed her and I knew she would always give me honest advice when I needed it or a shoulder to cry on during those times when I was younger and I felt as though my whole world was coming to an end, problems that were miniscule in comparison to those I'd face as I got older. She had a heart of gold and would help me out in any way she could. A true friend.

Both Ali and Jenna were outgoing and confident; similar in many ways. They both took anything that came their way with a pinch of salt. Ali couldn't give two hoots what people thought of her and enjoyed living life to the fullest. I was a little more reserved and more conscious of what people thought of me. Next to the two pretty and popular girls, I always looked at myself as being quite plain and boring and I suppose most other kids at school did view me as the odd one out of the three of us. But I didn't care, being with Ali was always an adventure and I enjoyed not knowing what the next day with her was going to bring whenever we were together.

The three of us remained close friends up until we got into our first year of college, where we slowly began to drift apart. Ali started to hang around with a new group of girls who were in the same drama course as her. Jenna and I also saw very little of one another. Finally, they both became just another face in the crowded college corridors to say a quick hello.

At eighteen, everything changed and my life was suddenly flipped upside down. A few months before my courses were due to finish, I was forced to drop out of college and a short while later my family and I moved away from Sandbroke permanently. By then, Ali, Jenna and I had lost contact almost completely. I heard from Jenna once, just before I moved away, to tell me she was moving to Bristol with her family, then I heard nothing else from her. Ali never bothered getting in touch at all, so neither did I. That's how things have stayed for a full fifteen years until now. *Why now?*

*

Half an hour later, the train pulls into Sandbroke station, I peer out of the window, memories already coming back in an abundance of emotion-filled flashbacks. As the train's doors open, passengers rush to grab their belongings and escape the uncomfortable confinement of the second class carriage. I'm itching to get off the train and stretch my legs after such a long journey, but I find myself frozen to my seat, still gripping onto the plastic cup of now cold coffee. The train hostess from earlier spots me and makes her way along the aisle, towards my seat.

"Everything okay there?" she asks, bending to eye level with me.

I need to move, I know I do. I have to do it for Ali. Slowly, I stand and gather up my belongings.

"Yes, fine," I manage. I steady myself and start walking shakily towards the open carriage doors. Carefully focusing on putting one foot in front of the other, I step out onto the platform and move towards the station exit. Then, I find myself on the once familiar Sandbroke high street.

I take in a long breath and hold it, the memories now running quicker than I can count as a wave of heat hits me like a solid iron wall. *Welcome back Emily.*

Chapter 3

There was only one place that I would even contemplate staying for my short trip back to Sandbroke. To be honest, apart from the cabin I had booked, there were only a couple of overly priced cottages in Sandbroke that were vastly out of my price range free for the dates I needed. When I hurriedly searched the Internet to find somewhere to stay after my call to the police department yesterday, there had been few small B&B's, but the only ones with rooms available at such short notice had been further out of town than I really wanted. The summer season has now started and Sandbroke has always been a popular thriving tourist spot. Although I haven't been back in years, I knew that Ceaders Holiday Park would still be going strong and it would provide me comfortable surroundings for my short stay. The log cabins are on the coast overlooking Ceaders Bay and were popular back when I had lived here. At the time, the holiday park was owned by a lovely lady called Maggie Donnelly. I called yesterday to make a reservation to learn that Maggie retired a year ago, but the park has now been taken over by her daughter Rose, who I remember was a few years older than me and attended the same senior school as I had. Luckily we didn't know each other well enough for her to remember me when we spoke, which I'm thankful for.

I start my walk from the train station only briefly taking in my surroundings as I go. I know that from here, the coast is approximately a fifteen-to twenty-minute walk. I could have taken the easy option and hailed a taxi outside the station, but my bag isn't too heavy and I could do with the fresh air to try and clear my pounding headache after being stuck on a busy train for almost seven hours.

I keep my eyes to the ground, only looking up in small glances to enable me to get my bearings, which come back to me at an amazingly quick speed. I see there has been some restoration work done in the town centre. New shops have sprung up that I don't remember, along with a few cafes, an Italian restaurant and a modern-looking pub on the corner of the high street that I'm sure used to be a post office. Although the small town has been updated, it still has the same layout as I remember and holds the same seaside village-feel charm it always did.

I'm sweltering hot as I reach the end of the small high street. It feels a lot warmer here than it did back at home. But then I am a lot further south in the country than I am used to now. The grey skies and cool drizzling rain that I left early this morning in the North East are very appealing at the moment. Already, I can detect a slower pace of life here, something that would in normal circumstances easily appeal to me. But now, I yearn for the fast-moving city crowds back at home that I can get quickly lost amongst.

I stop just before I reach the cabins and lean against a low dry stone wall attached to the side garden of a pretty pale pink painted cottage to catch my breath. I attempt to pull myself together before I go any further. Behind me, the cottage garden is alive with brightly coloured plants and flowers, the sweet smell of honeysuckle grips onto the air. Families with small children dot the pavements, all moving in the same direction. The children gleefully clutch onto buckets and spades heading home after an undoubtedly fun-filled day at the beach, away from the soft sands and shallow waters of Ceaders Bay. Taking off my thin cardigan, I wipe my brow on it and tie it neatly around my waist, then dig out a pair of sunglasses from the bottom of my unorganised handbag. Sliding them over my eyes, I briefly wonder if I am putting them on for the purpose in which they are intended or to try and mask my identity to some extent.

Immediately, the sun starts to burn into my exposed pale shoulders, and within a matter of minutes they begin to itch and turn red. I bend forward and bury my aching head in my hands. *What am I doing here? I swore I'd never come back.* A vision of Ali then enters my head and compels me to continue onwards.

There's a slight and highly welcome sea breeze as I head closer to the seafront and round the corner towards the holiday park. I pass the old church that my mum and dad had been married in, refreshingly unchanged by the amount of time that has passed by. Beyond it, the sea is a welcoming shade of bright blue merging seamlessly into the cloudless sky above. I can see the cabins now, a little further back perched in neat rows all identical in their auburn coloured wood and pretty white gloss painted windows. Shifting the rucksack on my back, which now seems to weigh far more than I do, I continue ahead and enter the small lodge at the park's entrance which houses the reception.

No one is here. There is a desk in the corner with a bell on it that I press hastily. I need to get out of these clothes and into a cold shower as soon as I possibly can.

"Hello there, sorry to keep you," says a woman. I look up from the desk to see that it's Rose Donnelly, rushing from outside to greet me behind the desk. Her wild red, curly hair and tiny frame haven't changed at all from what I remember.

"Hi," I say, as politely as my nerves will allow. "I have a booking."

"What's the name?" asks Rose. Thank God she hasn't recognised me. I'm really not in the mood for a catch-up. For once, I feel glad at the fact age has changed me so much.

"Emily Moore," I reply, hoping it still doesn't click. I rub at my sweating forehead.

"It's a scorcher isn't it?" Rose says, thumbing through a reservations diary.

"It certainly is."

"Yes, I have you here," she says, handing me a form to fill in and turning behind her to get a key. "You were lucky when you called yesterday. We only had the one cabin available. I guess it was meant to be." She smiles, as I slide the form containing my details over to her and she hands me the key.

"You're in cabin number seventeen," she says. "First road on your left and just follow it round. Enjoy your stay, Miss Moore."

"Thank you, I will," I mumble back. I know that I won't.

Throwing my bags to the floor as soon as I enter the cabin, I take a look around what I will be reluctantly calling my home for the next couple of days. I had been here a few times as a kid. I had never actually been inside one of the holiday cabins, however, and on first impressions am pleasantly surprised. It is a deceptively large space. Wooden from floor to ceiling with a small open plan kitchen in the corner and a stone-built open fireplace, surrounded by country cottage style furniture. Printed floral curtains hang at each of the large windows and matching canvas sofas fill the space. I continue to make my way through the cabin and discover that it has a large bathroom with a full-size roll-top bath tub and brass taps polished to perfection and two bedrooms both of which look out over the beach below boasting an unobstructed view of the ocean beyond. It would be a great place to stay if the circumstances were different. Lucy would love it, but I would never bring her here. How could I?

I don't waste any time hopping in the shower and changing. It's gone five p.m. now, and I want to get to the police station as soon as I can. I throw on a pair of shorts and the coolest, loosest-fitting top I have brought. There is no air-con in the cabin and the temperature feels stifling.

Leaving the cabin, I walk as quickly as I can through the holiday park. I make my way to the entrance following a winding gravel pathway edged by large grass verges. I pass a busy-looking clubhouse and a small swimming pool and kids play area that I recall never used to be there. The Donnellys really had done well with this place.

"Miss Moore." I hear my name and my heart catches in my throat when I realise it's a woman's voice shouting it. I turn to see it's just Rose, running over towards me from the reception lodge.

"I forgot to give you this." She hands me a small envelope with my name written across its centre. "It was handed in last week," she states.

"By who?" I ask, but I recognise the distinctive curly handwriting instantly and my heart skips a beat. It's from Ali.

"I don't know," replies Rose, pushing a stray curl behind her ear and adjusting her glasses. "It was left on the desk at reception. I didn't see who dropped it in, but I thought I'd hold onto it in case it was for a guest."

I manage a faint smile and nod. Slowly, I start to open the envelope as Rose smiles back and turns to walk away. Confusion bubbles inside of me. In the envelope is a key, just a single silver house door key with a sticky note attached:

Hi Em,
My address: 12 Ocean View, Cranley Quays. Please don't tell anyone.
Ali x

Chapter 4

Hot air blasts me full force in the face as I enter Sandbroke Police Station. I assume that the air-con here is non-existent too, just like back at the cabin. It's almost too hot to breathe. I walk slowly across the tiled floor attempting to keep my sandals from slipping from my hot and sticky feet. Apart from me, there's no one in sight.

"Hi, I'm Emily Moore," I say to the young pretty girl on the reception desk. "I'm here to see Inspector Mayland."

The girl looks up at me from her computer screen and nods. "Hi, Miss Moore. Yes, Inspector Mayland is aware you are coming, I'll just let her know you are here." She picks up a phone and points to a waiting area and smiles. "Please take a seat; she shouldn't be too long."

I head straight to the furthest corner nearest to both the open window and a large water dispenser. I fill a plastic cup and hold it to my lips. Only then do I notice I'm shaking. I use my other hand to steady the one holding the cup and take a sip. The water is warm as is the breeze coming through the fully opened window. Taking a seat on an old brown battered leather chair, I try to calm myself, but thoughts of Ali continue flashing through my mind. *Why does she want me to go to her house and not tell anyone about it? Is she really missing? Should I tell the police? What is going on?*

"Miss Moore." A woman's voice breaks my trance and makes me jump. Water from the cup spills onto my shorts and quickly soaks into the thin linen fabric. A tall, thin woman with shortly cropped, dark hair and pale skin stands in front of me.

"Inspector Mayland?" I ask, brushing off the droplets of water clinging to my shorts, a little embarrassed. I know already it is her as I recognise her voice from our phone call yesterday; she doesn't sound like she's from around here.

"Please, just call me Chrissy," she says, as she holds out her hand for me to shake. A now easy-to-distinguish Mancunian twang to her voice. "Thank you for taking the time to come all the way down here. Would you like to come through for a chat?"

I nod, wishing I could just turn around and head straight back out the door, catch the next train. I could be home by tomorrow if I left now. I could just give the police the e-mail, leave now, and forget this ever happened. But in my heart, I know I can't do that.

I follow Chrissy through to a large office space at the back of the building where there are lots of officers and staff around talking on phones, typing into computers, and scribbling furiously. Who would have known such small police department like Sandbroke would be kept so busy? Chrissy quickly spots my reaction the hive of activity surrounding us.

"They got rid of the Cranley station a few years ago along with a few other small stations in the district due to cutbacks. We do all of their work now too," she states casually.

"Oh," I reply, now understanding. "That's why they are dealing with Ali's disappearance in Cranley here?"

"Yeah, keeps us busy," Chrissy answers. "You said yesterday you're from Sandbroke originally?" she asks, genuinely interested.

"Yes," I answer softly. "I was born here."

"Must have been a nice place to grow up. I've only been here less than a year and love it already. Me and my husband moved here from Manchester for his job."

I smile politely, hardly hearing what she has just said to me.

"I was lucky enough to get a transfer here when I found out we would be moving. I was with Great Manchester police before."

"Really?" I ask, trying to show the interest her friendly attempts warrant.

"So, did you know Alison Martin well?" Chrissy continues through the large office and pauses at a desk to pick up a file that is resting on it. My eyes trail over the file. There's no name written on the front.

I snap back into focus. "Yes, a long time ago. Ali and I were best friends back when we were at school, but we lost touch over fifteen years ago."

Chrissy begins walking again, the file now tucked under her arm, which I assume must hold the information on Ali's case. I follow her, struggling to keep up with her long-legged fast pace.

"It's a little weird that she got in touch with me," I say, more to myself than to Chrissy.

"Not really," She replies. "Ali had only recently moved back to the area. Other than her mum, who passed away soon after she returned, it appeared she had very few friends here anymore."

"Oh, I see."

Chrissy leads me to a smaller, more private internal office with closed glass doors and plastic blinded windows looking out to the larger area. The office appears dated and in serious need of a revamp. Low ceilings and ridiculously bright lighting make the place feel overly oppressive.

"Have you heard anything else about Ali going missing?" I ask hopefully, entering the small office behind her.

"Yes, actually," replies Chrissy. "The local lifeguards in Cranley came forward with some of her belongings that had been abandoned on the beach the day that she appears to have gone missing."

"What, she had just left them there?"

"Seems so. They were handed in to them by a family who noticed nobody had come to collect them the whole time that they had been there."

"What sort of belongings were they?"

"Nothing out of the ordinary. Just the normal that you would expect anybody to take with them on a day at the beach, sunglasses, a towel, sunscreen, a change of clothes..."

"Surely they could have been anyone's. How do you know they were Ali's?"

"There was a book amongst her stuff. Had a dedication on the front page from the author made out to your friend. We are in the process of questioning the lifeguards on duty that day."

I nod back trying my best to process the information. My head spins.

"Would you like anything to drink?" asks Chrissy, as I take a seat near a tall electric fan and let the breeze hit me in the face. I follow it as it moves around its one hundred-and-eighty degree angle and back again. "I'm just waiting for my partner to join us. He should be here soon."

"Could I have a glass of water?" I ask desperately. I feel if I don't cool down I am going to pass out at any given moment.

"Of course." She smiles. "I'll be right back."

Chrissy leaves me alone in the office. I sit down behind the end of a desk of what I assume is one of her colleagues. A framed picture of a pretty blonde woman and two young boys wearing Sandbroke Primary School uniforms sits proudly on its edge. The colours of the uniform are still the same as when I went there, and the school logo attached to the front has only changed slightly from what I can remember.

A range of clutter and a mass of paperwork takes up the remaining three quarters of the desk's surface. A half-eaten service station sandwich has been left on top of a filing cabinet and what appears to be a gym bag and trainers rests next to it. *Whoever Chrissy's partner is must be a totally unorganised slob.*

I wait a few minutes before I hear the door behind me click open again. I turn expecting to see Chrissy, but it isn't her.

"Well, if it isn't little Emily Moore!" A deep voice fills the room, followed by a man moving so fast through the door that the breeze he brings with him causes some of the papers to blow from the desk and land at my feet. I study the man now in front of me as he bends to pick up the loose sheets, then turns back to me with a bright smile. He clearly knows and remembers me. I rack my brains and struggle to put a name to his face, but at this point in time I am unable to.

"I'm sorry… do I know you?" I ask, as politely as possible.

"It's Mark, Mark Logan," the man exclaims.

The penny quickly drops. "Mark!" I say, rising to my feet to give him a brief hug. "I'm so sorry, I didn't recognise you." I suddenly realise whose office it probably is that I'm in and instantly feel a little bitchy for thinking what I just had about its owner.

"Yeah, not exactly the trim young twenty-two-year-old stud you remember, eh?" he says, tapping on his slightly rounded belly, then rubbing at his once dark hair now streaked with silver. He's changed a lot over the years, but already, I can see he still has an air of endearing laddish charm that he possessed when he was younger.

"You became a cop?"

"I most certainly did." He points to a gold nameplate partially buried under a stack of folders, reading Chief Inspector Logan.

"Wow," I reply. I'm genuinely impressed by his high ranking. Of all the occupations in the world, I would never have imagined the laid back and relaxed Mark Logan to end up in the police force, and most definitely never in such a senior position.

Mark had been my sister's boyfriend all through high school. They were known affectionately back then as the town's childhood sweethearts. They stayed together through till when Trish left to live in Glasgow after she was offered a place in the university there. They stayed together for the first year of her four-year-long law degree, but the distance between them finally took its toll. Trish met her now-husband Max and promptly ended hers and Mark's relationship. I'd always really liked Mark, but I guess it just wasn't meant to be.

"God, how have you been?" asks Mark, taking a seat opposite me at the desk. "The last time I saw you, you could have only been a teenager."

"Nineteen," I confirm.

"How's Trish doing?" he asks. I detect a quick sadness flicker in his eyes, but it soon fades.

"She's good," I answer. "She still lives in Scotland. A lawyer in Glasgow. She's married now, with two daughters."

"She always did have a good head on her shoulders," Mark says, before tapping proudly at the family photograph on the desk that I had been admiring a few moments ago. "I've got two kids now, too."

I nod. "They're beautiful."

"And what about you?" he asks brightly. "Married? Kids?"

I feel myself grow anxious. The lies were going to have to come at some point. I didn't think it would be as early as this.

"No, no, not married. No kids." I shake my head uncomfortably, willing him to cease the questioning, a skill he's already proving he excels in.

"Really? It's a shame things didn't work out between you and Jake."

My breath catches causing me to cough and the room starts spinning around me. *Stay calm, stay calm.*

"No, no we went our separate ways a while back," I manage. My voice is shaking slightly so I choose not to elaborate further. I'm glad when Chrissy comes back into the room and breaks the awkward silence now surrounding us.

She hands me my drink and I swig the whole glass back in one.

"You've met my partner, Chrissy?" asks Mark, who seems to have noticed my sudden personality change and now looks a little uncomfortable himself.

"Yes," I say, as Chrissy sits down next to me and gives me a warm smile.

"Okay, shall we get started?" she asks Mark. I reach into my bag to pull out a copy of the e-mail from Ali.

"Yes," he replies, composing himself. He quickly makes a small space on the cluttered desk and somehow finds a pen and notepad amongst the chaos. He sits forward to look me in the eye, and then flashes me a reassuring smile.

"Let's find Ali."

Chapter 5

Hello again, Emily. It is so good to see you back in the place that we first met all those years ago. It felt so strange seeing you again after so much time has passed.

My, you've changed! I hardly recognised you when you stepped off the train a couple of hours ago at Sandbroke station. Where has that young, innocent girl gone? You have blossomed into a beautiful woman who holds herself with such poise and grace. Who would have known?

Of course, I could tell you were nervous and not acting quite like yourself. Who wouldn't be nervous, after all this time? It must have been difficult leaving your new life behind for a while to come back to your old one. For that, I must thank you.

You didn't see me as I watched you from afar as you struggled with your luggage in the blistering heat heading towards the holiday park. But then, I've changed too over time and probably look different than your memories of me. You looked lost and totally out of place walking through Sandbroke centre. Have you erased the memories of your hometown so easily that you couldn't even afford the time to slow down and take it all in? You made me feel exhausted just watching you.

I waited for a while and made sure I was hidden as you changed clothes in the cabin. I'm sorry if I scared you with the note. It really wasn't my intention when I wrote it, but I had to get it to you somehow and hoped that you would choose Ceaders cabins to stay while you are here to give me a way of getting it to you.

I watched you as you went into the police station and waited until you came out a little later. You took a while in there and I wondered what you were talking about with the police that took you so long. I'm not really too sure why you had to get them involved with the e-mail I sent to you, but that's fine. You are a good friend and I know that you are only concerned. I only hope they don't pry too much.

You looked a little happier when you left the station and then waited at the bus stop to catch the next bus to Cranley. There were no police with you. I take it you haven't told them about the key. As I knew you wouldn't. Take care, Emily. See you soon.

Chapter 6

It's approaching eight p.m. by the time I get to the small coastal town neighbouring Sandbroke where Ali's home is situated. Cranley Quays was only just starting to emerge as a reputable place to live when I left Sandbroke. Now it's classed as one of the most prestigious areas to reside on the English coast. Walking from the bus stop towards Ocean View I can see why.

Large mansion-type homes line the vast seafront, displaying luxury beachside living at the highest of standards. Fancy sport's cars and SUV's line up on long block-paved driveways next to extensive perfectly manicured gardens and green shapely lawns surrounded by tall wrought iron fencing.

Ali really had done well for herself if this is where she ended up. I know that she had gone on to be an actress and I had watched the TV drama series that she had starred in a couple of years ago religiously. She hadn't been in anything else since then, which I'm surprised at. She was a very talented actress, there was no denying that. I had no idea she had become so wealthy to be in a position to live in such a respectable area. I can't dismiss the feeling of jealously I have, when thinking of my own poky little two-bedroom flat back in the North East.

Rounding a corner, I make a turn onto the road that I know the address Ali has given me is based. It had been just a building site when I left Sandbroke, now it's a gleaming row of modern whitewashed houses looking out over the beach, not far from where the sand begins, leading down to a sea that today is calm and quiet. I count down the numbers until I reach number twelve. Standing back, I admire the huge box-shaped building in front of me surrounded by floor-to-ceiling gleaming windows. It looks like a work of contemporary modern art more than it does someone's home.

Quickly, I glance around to check there's nobody around and slide discreetly through a gate at the side of the property, which unexpectedly isn't locked; shoddy work on the authority's behalf, I imagine. Mark had told me earlier that the police had already done a full search of Ali's home, but nothing out of the ordinary had been found. However, I know that they could come back whenever they want. I need to be careful.

The key slips into the lock of the front door and slides open easily. Again, I am briefly astonished that there is not more security measures in place to protect such a beautiful home. I do another check up and down the road to ensure the coast is clear and swiftly move inside.

'Wow' doesn't even come close to accurately describe the entrance of Ali's home. I'm greeted by a huge hallway housing a massive low-hanging crystal chandelier. A grand staircase leads up to a first floor surrounded by a glass balcony. White walls are met by a white polished and spotless marble floor, which seems to flow throughout the whole house.

I hope that there will be no one here. Ali never married and didn't have any kids (so Mark told me) and I know she was an only child. She never knew her father and apparently her mum died six months ago. The police said there was nothing leading them to believe that she was in a relationship with anyone when she disappeared, but they couldn't be one hundred percent sure. At this early stage in the investigation, it appeared she had been living alone.

I let the door close quietly behind me and start to make my way through the house, choosing the living room first.

The huge room looks out over the sandy beach to the sea beyond, its view only temporarily interrupted by a small infinity outdoor swimming pool. Contemporary style decor and lavish soft furnishings dot the minimalistically-arranged room. Pieces of art work that I'm sure wouldn't look out of place in Paris's Louvre Museum are framed in heavy gold surrounds sporadically dotting the otherwise bare walls.

It's starting to get dark now; the room is bathed in a deep orange glow as the sun sets over the ocean. I don't turn on a light as I can't risk anyone knowing I was here, so I start to make my way around in the darkness. Ali wanted me to be here, maybe to find something. What, I have no clue.

I continue to look around the house and make my way into the kitchen. Its gleaming modern appliances look like they have been barely used and create a clinical type environment. I can't help but notice that the whole house feels totally impersonal. It could belong to anyone; there isn't an ounce of personality, love, or warmth in the place. I struggle to believe that this is the sort of home the flamboyant and glitzy Alison Martin—who had the biggest personality of anyone I have ever known—would have chosen to live.

Upstairs, I race through numerous rooms and have counted four perfectly dressed, but bland guest rooms that look as though they have never been used, by the time I reach what I assume is the master bedroom. This room is different. Instead of the neutral tones and sterilized feel that the rest of the house has, this room is unique and much more relatable to Ali's taste, as I remember it. The bedroom is decorated in bright pink shades and shiny metallics. Sparkly sequin-studded cushions dress the unmade king-size bed and blown-up family pictures in matching silver frames dot the main wall. Shoes lay on the floor in a neat row, a cream silk robe hangs on the back of the door, a pair of jeans and a T-shirt are folded neatly on a wicker chair in the corner. Her presence in the room is heavy, like she only just left it this morning and is yet to return.

Racing to the wall where the pictures are hanging, I scan the faces looking back at me. It's definitely Ali in the photos. Just the same much older and grown up version of Ali that I saw on the TV show she was in. Her once mid-length black curly hair is now a long, sleek and glossy style perfectly framing her beautiful dark almond shaped eyes. In some of the photos, her lips are stained in a bright pink lipstick that I had never seen her wear, but it suits her olive-toned skin. There's no doubt it's my old friend looking back at me.

The photos don't look recent, most maybe taken around five or six years ago judging by Ali's age. A few have her mother in them, who I recognise immediately. There a lot of Ali on her own posing in various famous landmarks around the world. Paris, New York, Barcelona, Honk Kong, Dubai. There's no denying she was certainly well travelled. There are two final photos as I move to the last of the collection. One is of Ali graduating drama school, posing proudly in a cap and gown, grasping a scroll in her hand. The other is of me, Ali, and Jenna from back in college. I take the photo from the wall and study it closely. I remember the day it was taken well. We are on Ceaders Bay. The sea partially covers our tanned bare legs where we stand posing for a photo with our arms around each other. Our faces are tanned and our eyes full of excitement. We look so young, full of fun, and carefree. It was the last summer we spent together. The summer I met Jake. I find myself wondering if this is proof that Ali cherished our friendship as much as I did.

Carefully, I replace the photo and leave to check the last of the rooms. Nothing seems strange or out of place just like Mark said, even Ali's wardrobe is perfectly ordered, everything in exact colour coordination, full of beautiful clothes and boxes of brand new designer shoes that I doubt have even been worn. The bathroom, as I expected, is filled with luxurious lotions and expensive bottles of perfume. I close the door, leaving it slightly ajar as it had been and turn to head back downstairs. If I hurry, I can catch the last bus back to Sandbroke. It's evident I've wasted my time coming here.

As I make my way down, something stops me. It's maybe just a hunch, but even so I need to check it out. I turn on my heel and head back to Ali's bedroom, something rapidly registering in the forefront of my mind. Racing back to the photo wall, I pick up the one of the three of us and run my finger around the edge of the frame where the prongs on its back are sticking up slightly, as though the back of the frame had recently been replaced and not secured properly. Quickly, I remove the back of the photo and run my hand around the rim, and sure enough inside behind a piece of cardboard is a small piece of paper folded into a neat square. *This is what she wanted me to find.* My hands trembling, I open the note and begin to read.

Hi Em,

Well done. I knew you'd find it. You always were the smart one! I have a lot to tell you. Meet me on Ceaders Bay tomorrow at 8 a.m. It will be quiet then, so no one will see me. Please don't tell anyone, especially the police. I know it's a lot to ask, but I can't risk it!

Ali x

Chapter 7

The orange glow of the sun rising streams in from the open window of the cabin, waking me from a restless night. I wake only for a few moments before drifting back to sleep again. The warmth like a comfort blanket wrapped tightly around me. When I had returned back from Cranley last night, I had taken a bath, watched a little television, and prepared myself some supper. I called Lucy and spoke to Mum and Dad assuring them that I was fine, but I think they could tell that I wasn't. Ali has been playing on my mind and not only that, but now Jake has been too. Could he still live nearby? I'm sure Mark would have mentioned it if he did.

I awaken again startled and promptly jump from the bed. The clock on the wall tells me it's seven-thirty. I'd better hurry if I'm going to get down onto the beach in time to meet Ali. I am anxious to see her and find out what is going on. She mentioned she was in trouble and I want to help her in any way I can.

I throw on a loose vest top and a pair of jeans. It looks as though it's going to be another scorcher today, the sky outside bright and cloudless already. I hastily throw my long hair into a bun at the nape of my neck in an attempt to stay cool and hurry outside in the warm morning air. I pass the maid, who smiles politely and says "Good morning," as she carries on along the pathway with her cleaning supplies in tow, as I rush past the other cabins. Rose is standing near her talking to one of the other guests and she waves to me and smiles as I pass her before continuing her conversation.

As Ali assured me in her note, the beach is deserted. I glance up and down the shoreline as I make my way along the sand. Slipping off my sandals, I roll up the bottoms of my jeans to my knees and head towards the south end of the beach where the rocks are. I let the water wash over my feet, and gasp as the cold hits my skin, foam bubbles around my toes as I continue on and the temperature becomes tolerable. I can't remember the last time I walked along a beach and let the ocean cover my feet like this. I miss living so close to the coast. It gives me a small feeling of freedom and leaves me, as always, questioning my tiny and insignificant part of this earth when faced head on with such an overwhelming specimen of nature's power.

As I near the large cluster of rocks, the strong odor of salt and sea kelp penetrates the air, making me once again think of the past. The rocks were the place I would always arrange to meet Ali and Jenna when we were younger, so I know this is where Ali will be today. I glance at my watch and sit down on a rock that is still slightly damp from the high tide. It's almost eight—she will be here soon.

The beach is peaceful this morning with only the sound of the ocean lapping at the shore and a few seagulls dancing at its edge as the sun continues its daily ascent into the sky. I remember being here during the summers as a teenager with

Ali and Jenna; lying on towels on the warm sand, admitting secrets to one another—usually based solely on the boys we fancied at school. I fight hard against images from a little later on in time, of me and Jake. The two of us all over each other when we first met, laughing happily as we skipped in and out of the water, our bodies close, stopping only briefly to kiss each other before the next wave broke. Before it all changed.

A lot of time passes, I'm not aware of how much until the nearby café staff start to bring out tables and chairs and set them on the wooden outdoor terraces preparing for the day ahead. It's almost nine a.m. and I am both worried and terrified at the fact Ali hasn't shown up. The beach starts to come alive with families out for a morning stroll and Sandbroke residents take their daily jog across the sand. I glance again at my watch—it's obvious she isn't going to show—Ali was never late, ever. She was ridiculously well organised and prepared. She was always the first to arrive anywhere we went. I doubt that would have been a part of her to change over time. *God, let her be safe.*

I stand from the rocks and brush the dried sand from my legs. My stomach grumbles and as I begin to walk I feel a little light headed. I had been unable to eat anything last night as I was in too much of a state. My supper had ended up being thrown in the bin back at the cabin. I am anything but hungry, but I know I must force myself to eat something; I'm no use to anyone feeling the way I do now. Grabbing my handbag, I head to the café and am greeted warmly by a waitress as I enter.

"Just take a seat. I'll be with you in a minute," the girl says in a friendly tone. I nod and head to a table near the window looking out directly onto the beach. The strong smell of freshly brewed coffee and sweet homemade cakes fills the air. I glance around at the large interior that no longer looks anything like it used to when I lived here. Inside, the place looks more like a trendy bar than the old rundown beach shack that it used to be. I remember it selling warm cans of soda, and the floor was always coated in a thin layer of sand, but it boasted the best fish and chips in miles. Now it is a fashionable-looking area dressed in decorative fisherman's nets, with smooth-carved wooden furniture surrounding a large glass bar in its centre stocking a vast array of wines and spirits. Old black and white photos are arranged on the wall showing Sandbroke's maritime history throughout the years. The waitress returns with a notepad and pen in hand and reaches to adjust her apron before greeting me.

"What can I get you?" she asks.

"Do you serve breakfast?" I ask, hoping she says yes. I don't have much food back at the cabin and don't relish the thought of having to go into the busy town centre.

"We do," she says, handing me a menu from a nearby table. I scan it quickly, bypassing the trendy options before ordering the plainest thing I can see—poached eggs with whole grain toast and a pot of English tea.

My breakfast arrives as the place starts to get busy. Families with small children begin to fill the tables surrounding me and cram into the small booths, the enticing smell of bacon and eggs now floods the air. I am staring out of the window finishing my pot of tea, deep in thoughts when a voice interrupts them.

"Mind if I join you?"

I look up to see Mark hovering over me.

"Mark, hi. Sorry, I was miles away. Please take a seat."

I study his smart uniform as he orders himself a coffee from the waitress he seems to be on first name terms with. I notice her eyes linger on him before she finishes taking the order, reinforcing the well-known fact that most women find it virtually impossible to ignore a man in uniform. He has a different look today when compared to the unshaven face and casual untucked shirt he wore when I met him at the station yesterday.

"Aren't you based at the station today?" I ask, pouring myself another cup of tea from the small silver pot in front of me.

"Just on my way in now," he answers. "I've been at a meeting, but just had to pop in and make the coffee run before I head back to the station."

"I can't get used to the idea that you became a cop," I say, pointing at his uniform lapels and giving him a playful shove. Time rewinds in my mind and I feel fourteen again, joking around with him like I used to.

Mark laughs. "I know, look at you sitting next to a real live policeman," he jokes.

"I'm honored," I say, smiling back. "They have you well-trained over at the station, then?" I nod at the coffee he's holding.

"They certainly do. Actually, I was hoping Tom would be here too." He looks around the place before setting his sights back on to me.

"Your brother?" I ask, knowing exactly who he is talking about and feeling my cheeks go a little red. Mark's younger brother Tom—or Tommy, as those lucky enough to know him well had called him back then—had been in my year at school. I'd had a mad crush on him for years, until Jake came along.

"Yeah, you remember Tom, don't you?" Mark asks me, flashing a grin. He knows full well how much I had liked Tom back in my teenage years; I have no doubt Trisha would have filled him in on all the details. I pick up my cup of tea and take a sip, trying to act casual.

"Are you meeting him here?" I ask.

"He should be starting work any time now." He glances at his watch.

"You've just missed him, Mark. He left early to pop to the suppliers," shouts the waitress from behind the bar, clearly eavesdropping into our conversation.

"Thanks, Tia," Mark shouts back over his shoulder.

"Oh, Tom works here?" I ask. I'm a little disappointed by the fact the intelligent straight A student that I had held such high hopes for had ended up as a bartender, but then I can't judge. I myself was a straight A student and had wound up in a similar type of profession as a waitress. The small city centre restaurant that I work in is a far cry from this place.

"He owns the place," says Mark. Pointing to the bar's name at the top of the menu resting on the table. 'Logan's Tavern.' I nod, all becoming clear.

"It's a great place," I admit, taking another look around.

"Yeah, it's really popular. But he's worked hard to get it to this point. It was a dilapidated mess when he first bought it. Tom and I inherited a little bit of money when our grandfather died. I blew mine on an expensive car and a few luxurious family holidays. Tom, being the sensible one of the two of us, invested his share into buying this place when it went up for sale a couple of years ago. The rest, as they say, is history."

I smile.

"So when you are heading back home?" asks Mark, clearly maneuvering the conversation away from his younger brother.

"Later today," I answer, feeling a large stab of guilt in my chest. "I only came down here to show you guys the e-mail and see if I can be of any help. But it seems you have everything under control. Besides, I have to get back to…" I trail off and stop myself abruptly before saying 'my daughter.' I had already told Mark yesterday that I don't have kids and I don't want to confuse the situation. This is a small town and news travels fast. Although I'd like to tell Mark the truth, I can't risk word getting back to Lucy's father. "Get back to my job," I add quickly, feeling myself grow anxious.

"I see." Mark studies my face before reaching for his coffee.

"Have you heard anything more about Ali?" I ask, hopeful that someone has come through with some information as to her whereabouts.

"No. Chrissy is leading the team in doing some more door-to-doors in the area this afternoon to see if anything new has come up, but like I told you yesterday she seemed to have become a very private person. Nobody knew a lot about her. No family that we know of and no friends."

"So, which neighbour reported her missing?" I ask. "She must have let that person into her life, at least."

"It was her next door neighbour, Mrs. Robertson. Well, if you can class it as 'next door.' All the houses around Cranley Quays are pretty far apart." I nod, acting like this is news to me. "Ali walked Mrs. Robertson's dog for her on a daily basis. When Ali didn't show up for three days solid, she became worried and called us. To be truthful, we all thought Mrs. Robertson was probably a little mixed up. She's eighty-two and let's just say her mind isn't as young as it once was."

"But Mrs. Robertson was right?"

"She was. If it hadn't been for her calling us nobody would have known any different. Nobody would have even noticed Ali had gone." Mark glances out the window thoughtfully.

"Did you find out where the e-mail she sent to me came from?"

"Yeah, it was sent from her own home computer. Her e-mail account had barely been used in recent years, apart from that one message sent to you."

"What about phone records. Can you access them?" I realise now I'm asking questions I should have asked Mark and Chrissy yesterday at the station, but I was so flummoxed at the time we ended up discussing very little.

Mark shakes his head. "The department is still looking into them now. Her home phone line was only connected after her moving six weeks ago, and has only been used to call two numbers, both of which were just local Chinese takeaways. Didn't seem she was a big fan of cooking." Mark smiles, trying to lighten the mood before he continues. "We have a record of the calls you made to the number and the messages you left on her machine, but nobody else called her on it."

"Not that surprising. I hardly use my home phone either and I've had mine for years," I offer.

Mark nods. "She didn't have a mobile registered to her, but could possibly have a pay-as-you-go phone that she used for the majority of her calls. The phone and all her debit and credit cards must be with her as they weren't in the house when we searched. We've found no suspicious activity on any bank accounts registered to her, up to now."

Mark looks a little uncomfortable and I know that I need to stop with the questioning as he has most likely told me far more than he should on a professional level.

I really need to tell him about the note Ali left for me, but I don't dare. Ali swore me to secrecy and there's a reason she doesn't want the police involved. Mark must notice the look of anguish on my face.

"We're trying our best, Em, but the fact she was such a private person isn't helping with the case. I'm sure we will find her. I have my best team on the job they won't leave any stone unturned. It's still relatively early days." He rises to his feet, draining the last of his coffee from his mug before squeezing me on the shoulders reassuringly.

"Thanks for coming down Em, it was good to see you. I've got your number, I'll be in touch as soon as we hear anything." I nod, feeling useless and tremendously guilty for leaving. As Mark turns towards the bar to pick up his take out order, his mobile phone starts to ring he reaches inside his trouser pocket quickly answering the call.

"Hi Chrissy, yeah, I'm just coming back now… Yes, I see… I'm on my way." Mark finishes the call and turns to face me again, he looks shaken. I'm already on my feet.
"That was Chrissy." Mark begins to dial another number into his phone as he flings some money on the bar and picks up his car keys. As he moves toward the door leading to the back car park of the bar, I chase after him.

"What is it Mark?" I ask, unsure if I really want to hear the answer.

"There's been a body found washed up on the beach fifteen miles south of here in Pemblington," he answers, as he reaches his car and opens the door. "They think they've found Ali."

Part Two

Chapter 8

Sandbroke was unusually quiet the summer I met Jake, with a lot of its normal annually returning tourists taking up on the tempting deals from low cost airlines offering no frills flights to the Spanish Costa's and beyond; they had recently started to boom in business.

It was a cloudy day, but mild. An invisible energy hung in the air, hinting that bad weather could possibly be on its way. Outside the sky was dull, the streets hauntingly quiet at the height of the summer season. I was in an American style diner, which was on the high street back then. The place only lasted a few months before it was refurbished back to a country style tea room that seemed to go down much better with both the residents of Sandbroke and holiday makers alike. I had recently broken up for the summer holidays after finishing my final year of high school a few weeks earlier and was excited about what the approaching weeks would bring. Jenna and Ali were with me. The three of us messing around, giggling and laughing, lost in our own private jokes, as we always were back then. Jenna was sipping on a chocolate milkshake, Ali enjoyed a huge vanilla ice cream covered with multi-coloured sprinkles, while I nursed an iced tea. I think that was my attempt at coming across as grown up and sophisticated back then. I didn't really enjoy the taste. Never have.

Ali was busy telling us about a drama school that she was interested in getting into after finishing college and Jenna was telling her she should go for it. I made an escape to go outside to get some air and some quiet for a bit. Although I loved Ali to bits, sometimes she spoke about nothing but herself. Unlike Jenna, I wasn't prepared to massage her ego any more than I had already that day. I was to my limit, so I decided to leave them to it for a little while. I knew Jenna secretly liked it when it was just her and Ali; I always had the sense that she was a little jealous of the bond that I had with her.

I squeezed out of the red leather booth. My trainers squeaked against the ridiculously unsubtle black and white checked flooring as I made my way to the door of the diner. That's when it happened—the best moment of my life then, and with hindsight, the worst now. The moment I met him.

As always, I wasn't looking where I was going, staring at the ground. Before I knew it, I had walked straight into him. I smashed hard into his chest, sending him backwards, the coke he was holding sloshed onto him, quickly soaking through his clothes.

"I'm really sorry," I said, finally looking up. I think my mouth almost certainly visibly fell open. He was tall, like me, with a mess of golden floppy hair and bright blue eyes. I was transfixed from the first moment I saw him. *Mistake number one.*

"It's okay, don't worry about it," he said, rubbing at his wet, brown-stained T-shirt with his tanned hand. I flushed, embarrassed, and could vaguely hear Ali and Jenna giggling hysterically from the booth behind me.

"Let me buy you another one," I replied, fidgeting in the back pocket of my jeans to find the loose change that I knew was in there somewhere. Swiftly, he moved his hand and touched my arm to stop me dead in my tracks.

"Why don't you buy me a drink tonight instead?" he asked casually.

"Um… um." My words wouldn't come out.

He laughed. "I take it that's a yes," he said. I nodded back, managing a smile of sorts.

"Brilliant, then that's sorted. I'll meet you here tomorrow night at seven. Is that alright for you?"

"Yes. Great," I blurted back instantly, feeling taken aback, but undoubtedly impressed by his undeterred confidence and forwardness. He carried on walking towards the door and I turned to head back to the girls, who were now dead silent, clearly gobsmacked at what they had just witnessed. I was grinning from ear to ear like a Cheshire cat.

"Oh, what's your name?" he shouted from behind me. As I turned back, he flashed me a smile that made me go weak in the knees.

"Emily," I said, a little more self-assured now that I was back at the table with my friends.

"Nice to meet you Emily. I'm Jake. See you tomorrow night."

Chapter 9

That first date with Jake was nothing short of amazing, as much as it pains me to say that now. We met outside the diner as planned and headed straight to a little wine bar on the seafront near Ceaders. I wore a bright red dress, borrowed from Ali, and it hugged tightly to my thin frame. It was much more daring than anything I would have chosen for myself, but Ali talked me into it using her powers of persuasion that never failed to succeed on me. My long mousey hair was curled, hanging down to my waist, and I had far too much makeup on in the hopes that I would get into the bar without question and they would serve me unaware that I was underage. I was only sixteen at the time, but unfortunately wasn't unfamiliar with bars and drinking culture. Ali, Jenna, and I would regularly catch the train to Cranley on a Friday night and sneak into its beach club, which was always filled with teens, most of whom we knew from school. My mum and dad would have killed me if they had known, but they never found out. We would all cover for each other and were never rumbled. To this day, my mum and dad don't know about it.

Jake was wearing a leather biker jacket and faded denim jeans. I remember thinking how cool he looked and I felt honored to be seen even standing next to him. The small wine bar was cramped and I had no choice but stay close to Jake. I could feel the heat from his body coming through his thin T-shirt as I sipped on my white wine and tried to hide my nervousness.

We told each other a little about ourselves, starting with the basics, then later moving on to more detailed and personal information. I learned that he had only recently moved to Sandbroke. He was a bricklayer by trade and had been offered a long-term contract on the new housing developments that had started in Cranley. His family lived in Manchester and he didn't really know anybody outside of work in the area yet; appeared I was the first. He had been living in Sandbroke for almost three months, already loved it, and had recently rented a one-bed flat on a road I knew well just off the main high street. I told him that I was starting college in September and had decided to study business, because that's the course that would lead to Uni and make me the most money which was the thing that really mattered in life to me then. I told him my real passion was art. My all-time dream was to paint landscapes in watercolour for a living. I hoped to one day make enough money to buy my own studio and sell my work to people who loved to get lost in a painting as much as I did.

People kept nudging me and shoving to get past where I was standing, pushing me more and more off balance until I eventually fell onto him. Embarrassed, I attempted to push myself away, but as I began to move, Jake's arm slid around me pulling me closer. It was effortless, his hand rested in the dip of my lower back like it was always meant to be there. He tilted my chin towards him and kissed me right there in the middle of the busy bar. I'd kissed boys before, but never like this, and although he was only a few years older than I, his experience shone through. I craved more.

Later, we moved on to another bar, had a few more drinks and laughed and danced together, until finally I loosened up and started to enjoy myself. It was one of the best times of my life.

That night we went back to his flat and we slept together. It's something I swore I'd never do. I hardly knew him, and it was so out of character for me. Until that point, I had been a virgin, possessing no sexual experience and outrageously romanticized plans of how my first time would be. Jake was gentle, as if he knew how nervous I was. From beginning to end it felt so right and I decided at that moment that I wanted to spend the rest of my life with this man. Even though I knew very little about him, I felt a connection to him that I couldn't deny.

*

The first few months that Jake and I were together were blissful. We spent every waking moment with each other and I could feel myself falling deeper and deeper for him. Jake soon convinced me that I should follow my dreams and I decided that he was right. I quickly made the decision to listen to what my heart told me and changed my course at college to study art instead of the business course that I hated. I loved him even more for encouraging me and wanting me to be happy.

We had been together for a little while when I moved in with him. By that time I was almost eighteen, and although my parents were a little worried, they had met Jake and approved of him. He had charmed them the same way that he had charmed me. I started to see less and less of Ali and Jenna, investing all of my time into Jake. After all, he was the ideal man for me and had started to become my new best friend. He had admitted he didn't really like it when I spent so much time away from him with my friends. I didn't mind; after all this was the man I would marry and grow old with. He was perfect. But as we all know, people can change as time passes, and unfortunately for me, Jake was one of them and things soon took a drastic turn.

Chapter 10

It didn't take long for our relationship to turn sour. It's hard to believe that something once so pure and beautiful could turn into something so poisonous, so fast, but sadly, it did.

I ditched college with less than five months remaining for my art course, much to the dismay of both my college lectures and my parents. My grades at college had been consistently high and I had been predicted overall fantastic grades by my tutors, gaining me entry to a vast choice of art schools and universities. The lecturers said I had a real eye and told my parents they thought I would make a fantastic artist one day. I dismissed the praise and their constant protests against my seemingly out of the blue decision to quit. I was now aware I was wasting my time following false hopes and had to focus instead on real life. I told myself that I needed to set my sights on getting a job that would pay the bills and let go of my unrealistic childhood dream. My parents were annoyed with me because they felt I had thrown away a future with great prospects. Something inside of me had changed and I didn't have the same ambitions I once had. My future wasn't going to work out the way I had once planned, and I didn't care because as long as I was with Jake nothing else mattered.

I soon started working at the local pub, but that didn't bring in much money and Jake was spending almost all the salary he brought in, so I picked up a second job as a waitress in the café which had previously been the diner where Jake and I had first met.

It started with the drinking. Jake would go out more and more and I found myself going out less and less. I spent almost every night alone watching the clock and wondering what time he would choose to roll in. I had grown apart from Ali and Jenna completely by then, and we had now all gone our separate ways. I had even pushed my family away and saw very little of them. I grew increasingly more alone and isolated. All I seemed to do was work and the small amount of spare time that I had, I didn't have the energy to even try living life in the way that I should have back then. I hated him for forcing me to miss out on my late teenage years that should have been some of the best of my life and I hated me for allowing that to happen. I won't ever get that time back.

Jake's drinking soon got out of hand. He was sacked from his job in Cranley and seemed to have no drive or motivation to get another. He continued drinking on a daily basis and seemed to spend best part of his time nursing a hangover or possibly in a police cell sobering up with multiple charges under his belt for being drunk and disorderly and disturbing the peace. He soon developed a reputation for himself and became a regular gossiping point for the town. He began to treat me like dirt and all we did was argue. Yet still, I didn't say anything and I didn't leave him. I lost the person that I was and my own identity seemed to be shadowed by his.

Months passed, and soon I had been with Jake for almost two years. On our second anniversary of the day we first met at the diner, I found out he had been cheating on me. Admittedly, it came as no shock, but still, I was heartbroken. I confronted him about it and he didn't deny it at all; in fact he bragged. He told me she was a girl who worked for the company he was once employed by, that he had been seeing her for a while. She was as sexy as hell and turned him on in ways I had never even come close to. I was devastated, and this time, I left him immediately. I packed my bags and headed straight back to my parents who, of course, welcomed me back with open arms.

Jake pleaded with me for weeks to go back to him. He called me, followed me. Wherever I went it seemed Jake just so happened to be there too—it became almost obsessive. When nothing worked, he finally gave up the drink and seemed to get himself back on the straight and narrow and even managed to get his job back. He promised me he was a changed man, and like a fool, I was naive enough to take his word for it. I moved back in with him a short while later, much to the consternation of my family. For a while things were back to normal, but then the drinking started again, only this time it was even worse.

Jake only hit me once, but once was all it took. I loved him with all my heart and had now endured over two years of verbal abuse and emotional torture. When I found out that he was cheating on me again and I threatened to leave him, he lost it and slapped me across the face. This time, I knew it was over for good. From somewhere within me I found strength and finally started to see that I was worth more than what I was putting up with. But, just like the first time, he wouldn't leave me alone, pleading with me to go back to him and telling me that his life wasn't worth living if I wasn't in it. After a couple of months of constant hounding and an eventual police restraining order, the harassment finally stopped. But I couldn't settle, how could I? I knew that he lived in the same small town and I could easily bump into him wherever I went. As long as I lived in Sandbroke there was no way I would be able to live my life to the fullest, in fear of always having to look over my shoulder. So, when my dad was offered a job near Newcastle upon Tyne, it seemed the logical option to go with them. I never heard from Jake again.

A short time after moving to the North East, I found out I was pregnant with Lucy. I was nineteen and a single mum, to say I was frightened would be an understatement, but there wasn't a single second that I considered not having my baby, nor did I ever consider telling Jake he was a father. He didn't deserve to be a parent and he certainly wasn't having anything to do with my daughter. My parents and sister, Trish, were more than amazing and to this day they have been the most supportive and loving family I could ever wish for. As for Lucy, I love my daughter more than anything in this world. I've lied to her about her father to protect her. She believes that he didn't want to be part of our lives and I thank God that up to this point she has never questioned his whereabouts or even craved for a lot of detail about him. She is happy, and that is all I could ever wish for.

I don't know what happened to Jake Saunders. I don't know what he did with his life, what he looks like now, or even where he ended up living, nor do I care. All I know for sure is that I never want to have to see him again for as long as I live.

Part Three

Chapter 11

The drive to Pemblington normally takes just over half an hour. But on this occasion, it seems more like twelve. I'm overly aware that I really shouldn't be here, but I'd insisted I accompany Mark on the journey. I couldn't have stayed at Logan's twiddling my thumbs and done nothing. Once again, Mark is bending the rules more for me than he should be. He tries his best to make small talk during the journey, even staying clear of any personal questions, but even he is much quieter than normal, which is maybe for the best as I can't fully focus on him. I need to know if in fact my old childhood friend, the one of only two best friends that I have ever had in my life, is dead.

Heat blazes through the open car window of Mark's large and expensive-looking Mercedes. He has the air con on full, but I need fresh air in my lungs to try and stop the nausea brewing inside my stomach. I've already had to ask Mark to pull over once because I felt so sick. *Maybe breakfast wasn't such a good idea.* Mark's busy muttering on about something to do with the performance of his car. I hear a few tangled words like 'horse power' and 'cylinders' which I presume are linked to the topic he has chosen to discuss. He sounds as if he's trying to keep his own mind off the now rapidly approaching event in front of us. At any other time, I would be interested in Mark's car, with its fancy-looking interior and hip gadgets that surround an incredibly complicated looking on board computer. My dad is massively into cars and his influence over the years has caused both my sister and me to be well on our way to be worthy of the title of 'petrol heads.' Today, I couldn't care less.

As we shoot forward along the busy road, small coastal villages whiz by, most of which are so small that I can't even count to ten before we pass through and leave them behind. We leave the route shortly hitting the quieter country roads I remember well, that twist and turn as views of the ocean momentarily disappear before coming back to produce an idyllic post card-type scene.

I had been to Pemblington numerous times for family day trips when I was younger; it had been one of my parents favourite weekend getaways. It was a pretty village dotted with white cottages with thatched roofs shadowed by the ruins of an old castle perched high and proud on a hill in its centre. Up to this point in my life, I have nothing but fond memories of the place, but I feel today that will come to an end.

"You alright?" asks Mark. We pass under the castle's shadow, creating a split second of darkness in the car as the sun is blocked by the domineering structure. I can't help feeling his question is nothing less than utterly stupid at this moment. We are, after all, heading to the location of my best friend's body.

"Fine," I answer abruptly.

"You didn't have to come, you know. I would have called you as soon as I found out if it is Ali," he replies in a similar tone to match my own.

"I know, I wouldn't have settled though," I whisper back. "I just need to know, Mark."

"You don't have to wait much longer." Mark hits the brakes a little too heavily, and I jolt forward in my seat. "We're here," he says coldly.

We pull onto a gravel public car park overlooking the shores of Pemblington Bay. It is exactly the same as I remember, back when Trish and I used to play here when we were young, unscathed by the years that have passed by. A perfect golden shoreline stretches out for miles, the castle walls loom in the distance.

Already, I can see a small white tent close to the water's edge. I had only ever seen one on TV crime drama series' much like the one Ali used to star in. I don't know a lot about the procedure surrounding them, but I know enough to work out that a corpse will more than likely be inside.

Mark takes off his sunglasses and places them on the dashboard before he reaches out to open the car door.

"I won't be long. Why don't you get some fresh air? It'll do you good, you look pale," he says. I nod up at him, unable to speak back.

I watch Mark as he makes his way down to the sea, greeting a couple of police officers on his way and stopping at a smart-suited man who is busy talking into a police radio. He says something to Mark and they both glance towards me. I get out of the car shakily and move to a cobbled wall overlooking the beach where police tape sections off the best part of the sand. Sunrays eat into my bare arms, making me feel queasy. I watch as a small crowd of teenagers gather near me, pointing to the activities taking place on the beach. What is it with the human fascination with such awful events? It's morbid.

There's a slightly stronger wind here today than there is further along the coast. The sea looks calm, just as it did earlier back in Sandbroke, but I know well of the hidden currents that swell invisible under its surface. It's a warning I had embedded into me from the time I was young and a reason this part of coastline doesn't go long without the odd fatality rearing its ugly head. What if Ali had decided to go for a swim that day she was at the beach in Cranley? What if the already over-stretched, overworked lifeguards failed to see her entering the water on an undoubtedly crowded beach? I remember her to be strong and fearless swimmer when she was younger. What if she got into trouble and nobody was around. Or, what if she was never in the water before she died. What if someone put her there? What if that is the trouble she was in. The reason that she needed to speak to me so urgently. *Was someone after her?*

I watch silently as Mark waits until the suited man finishes talking on the radio, shakes his hand, and follows his lead to the tarpaulin. My heart hammers in my chest. I want to stand up and get closer but I fear my legs won't support my weight. I lean forward and bury my head in my hands. *God this can't be happening.*

When I lift my head, Mark has already emerged from the tent and is heading back towards me. I can't tell yet by the look on his face what the verdict is. The little colour that he had in his cheeks has gone and I wonder after so many years of being on the force having to do this still has a profound effect on him. I suppose he wouldn't be human if it didn't. I bow my head back to the ground, preparing myself for the worst. *I can't do this.*

Mark reaches me quickly and takes my hand, slowly I lift my head to look at him.

"It's not her, Em," he says, relief shows on his face.

"Oh," I manage, feeling terrible for appearing so grateful when another young woman's life has been taken in such a terrible way.

"The woman was around the same age as Ali but apart from that there was absolutely no resemblance. Police are looking into possible missing cases now; she could have come from anywhere along this stretch of coastline. Ali seemed like the most plausible explanation, but seems not."

I grip my hands together in tight fists and bite my lower lip in an attempt to prevent myself from crying.

"Come on, let's get you back to Sandbroke." Mark rubs my shoulder and guides me back to the car where I settle into the seat feeling suddenly drained.

We start the drive back to Sandbroke and I'm actually starting to relax a little when my mobile phone alerts me to a text message, and I suddenly realise I haven't texted Lucy to say good luck for her final exam at school today. I unlock the phone, feeling like the worst mother in the world for forgetting such an important event in my daughter's life to date. But the message isn't from Lucy. It's from an unknown number. I slide the button to read it as Mark pulls off the gravel car park.

It only has three words printed across the screen in capital letters:

I'M STILL ALIVE

*

Mark drops me back at the holiday park. A little later, I head to the supermarket in the town centre, where I mindlessly whiz around the aisles as quickly as I can to pick up necessary supplies to take back with me to the cabin. I've decided to stay on in Sandbroke another night, rather than head back home today as I had originally intended. I feel too exhausted by the events of the last few hours to even contemplate travelling. Lucky for me, the cabin is vacant until the weekend.

The drive back to Sandbroke from Pemblington Bay with Mark had been almost as quiet as the drive there. He was as deep in thought as I had been, and I found myself wondering again if the job has taken its toll on him the way I knew it would me. He told me he has been in the police force for over thirteen years now. He has seen a number of bodies throughout his career, but I'm sure that it doesn't get any easier with time. He's gone back to the station to update Chrissy and the team, but promised me he will call if he hears anything else about Ali.

The walk back to the cabins helps to calm me down a little and I am once again relieved that I didn't bump into any old Sandbroke residents who remember me. A picture of Ali printed onto posters surround me as I leave the high street. Her pink painted lips and beautiful brown eyes copied from the same photo I had seen on her bedroom wall smile out from shop windows and lamp posts, appealing to anyone who has seen her since her disappearance or knows anything about her.

It's starting to get dark by the time I get back to the holiday park. I'm annoyed that most of my time today has been wasted following a false lead when it could have been spent helping to find Ali. Then I feel amazingly selfish, when I think about the poor dead girl's family who will undoubtedly soon be traced and told the devastating news of their deceased loved one gone far too soon. It's a cruel world.

Entering the holiday park, I make my way through the winding paths towards my cabin. The carrier bag that I'm holding is starting to cut painfully into my hand so I pick up my pace. I pass families and couples heading towards the clubhouse and nod to greet them politely as I pass. I'm almost at the corner of the row where my cabin is based when I see her.

She sits on a swing in the children's play area. It's difficult to see at first because it is so dark, but I can tell it's her. I drop my bag to the ground. Contents fall onto the grass and I hear a small cracking sound as the half dozen eggs I have just purchased make contact with the gravel. I look around me. There is no-one in sight; the music from the clubhouse has now disappeared as the wind has changed its direction. Now all I can hear are the waves in the distance and the creaking sound of the metal hinges that hold the swing she is sitting on. She has her head to the ground looking at the play bark that covers the area.

"Ali," I shout, but it's not loud enough for her to hear me with the distance between us. I head towards her not allowing myself to take my focus from her. As I get nearer, I can see in the dimming light that she wears a blue blouse that I remember seeing in one of the photos back at her house. It's a memory that comes back to me easily because it's the identical shade of Lucy's eyes. Her long black hair hangs sleek and loose resting on her knees. She doesn't see me and continues to swing slowly back and forth. The creaking of the swing becomes louder as I approach.

I'm almost at her when a young couple emerges from a nearby cabin. They have their arms around each other, the man says something and the woman giggles loudly. Ali's head snaps up as she realises there are people near her, and she quickly gets up from the swing.

"Excuse me, can you tell me where the nearest place is we can get something to eat?" The man asks, his attention focused on me.

"Erm…," I watch as Ali begins to run away from the kids' play area and I start to jog after her. "Logan's down on the beach," I shout, as I move past the young couple to follow in the direction that Ali has run in.

"Cheers," says the man as he throws a thumb into the air.

I continue to run, but by the time I reach the swings Ali has disappeared. I look left and right, shouting her name, then frantically rotate in a full circle, but I know instantly that it's too late. The wind picks up its speed sending my hair up around my head. I pull my jacket around me tightly, feeling a sudden coldness run through my entire body as I look out into the darkness.

Ali has gone.

Chapter 12

"So you think it was definitely her you saw tonight?" asks my sister.

"I think so, yeah. I'm totally confused to be honest, Trish," I answer. I squint at the full moon, perched high above the dark, black ocean. The howling wind knocks at the cabin windows. I reach to tilt the blinds in front of me and shut out what has turned into a dreary and miserable night.

I've been on the phone to Trish for almost half an hour now. She called me wanting to know what had happened after she had spoken to my parents who had told her I was staying on another night in Sandbroke. I hadn't gone into full detail with my parents. I know how much they worry about me and they don't need any added stress. Instead, I have vented off all my frustrations to Trish, who is now as thoroughly mystified about the whole situation as I am.

"I really think you need to tell Mark that you think you've seen her, Em."

"I know I should, but the one thing that Ali asked me not to do is tell anyone, especially the police. There must be a reason for that, Trish. If I tell them it might make things worse."

"But if you've seen her, she's not technically missing anymore."

"I know, but she still hasn't returned home, so something isn't right."

"And it's definitely her that sent you the note?"

"Yes, it was written in her handwriting. It's never changed."

"It's just so weird… but she seems okay, she isn't hurt in any way?"

"I think so. When I saw her earlier tonight she seemed fine, so at least I know she hasn't been harmed. But she doesn't want anybody to see her for some reason, which is maybe why I think she didn't show up at the beach this morning and why she scarpered before."

"What about the body found on Pemblington Bay today, is there any link there?"

"Nope. Just a pure coincidence. Mark had a phone call when we got back to Sandbroke saying that a surfer was reported missing in Cranley. Looks like it could be her."

"Poor girl." Trish sighs and pauses, considering. "And nobody in the area had any contact with Ali?"

"No, doesn't look like it. She had been living in London for seven years back when she was acting. She only had her Mum here."

"Is that why Ali came back there?"

"Yeah, I think so. Mark said she came back here six months ago and Sandra died a few weeks later."

"That's a shame, I remember Sandra was a nice woman." Trish sighs. "So Ali was a bit of a loner then?"

"Seems that way, yeah."

"I find it really hard to believe, she was always such an outgoing kid. It seems strange for her to turn into an outsider."

"Apparently it's true. The police questioned some of the people she worked with in London but nobody has seen or heard from her since she left to come back to Sandbroke." I recite the updated information Mark gave me before I left him today. I'm grateful that he is being so honest and keeping me fully briefed on the case. It's a shame I can't return the favour and be truthful with him too.

"Do you think Ali is still in some sort of trouble? The same trouble she mentioned in the e-mail she sent you?"

I rub at my aching temples, then take a sip of orange juice, pushing the half eaten slice of overdone toast and cold vegetable soup to the side. "I don't know, Trish. Maybe. I have an awful feeling about all of this. I hope I'm wrong."

A loud knock at the door makes me jump. At the same time I hear Max—Trish's husband—mumble something on her end of the line. I vaguely make out the noise of one of their daughters crying in the background.

"Trish, I have to go. There's someone at the door, I'll call you tomorrow, okay?"

"Yeah, me too. Okay, Em, look after yourself and please be careful. Text me before you go to sleep."

"You too, I will. Bye, Trish."

I try not to let myself get emotional over my sister's concern. Trisha has always fulfilled her role as an overprotective older sister and worries continually over my safety. She hates it when she knows I'm anywhere alone. The fact that I am alone and back in Sandbroke only makes it worse.

I cancel the call and pop my mobile back into my pocket before jogging to answer the door. What if it's Ali? God, I hope it is. She could have come back once nobody was around. I swing the door open hoping to see her, but it's just one of the holiday park's employees.

"Hi, Miss Moore. I was told you are staying on for another day with us. I was just going to drop these in for you. I'm Claudia, I help out with the housekeeping for the cabins."

The young-looking girl smiles pleasantly and hands me a couple of large fluffy white towels with a small selection of toiletries perched on top.

"I'll come first thing in the morning and do a full clean," she adds.

"Thank you," I say, as she turns and leaves. One thing I certainly can't knock here is the service.

I take the towels straight through to the bathroom and decide to take a hot shower. Drawing the blinds, I strip off and enter the walk-in cubicle. The stream from its flow immediately starts to clear my cloudy head. As I soap over me and wash my hair, thoughts go through my mind at a thousand miles per hour. Mark, Chrissy, Ali, Jenna, Jake, the poor dead girl on the beach today. *What is going on?*

I exit the shower and pick up the towel from the floor; the bathroom is filled with the scent of lavender scented soap and aromatherapy oils. I inhale deeply and rotate my still tense shoulders, but I know relaxation at the moment would be nothing short of a miracle. The towel is still neatly folded, I quickly unravel it and wrap it around myself. As I do this, something on the floor at the front of the cabin catches my eye through the gap in the bathroom door. Securing my towel, I make my way to the entrance to discover the item on the floor is a large piece of paper. I bend to pick it up, assuming it must be Claudia's. But as I turn the paper I realise it's not something of Claudia's at all. It's one of the posters appealing for Ali that I saw in the town centre earlier. The photo of Ali alone sitting on a picnic blanket placed on a bright green grassy area, her lips painted bright pink dominates it.

My hand trembles as I turn to read the words written on the back of the poster in thick black marker pen. The same curly neat handwriting as in the note yesterday:

Friends Forever

Chapter 13

My hair is still dripping wet and matted as I run through the holiday park and towards the reception lodge. Rose looks a little taken aback by my appearance when she sees me enter. She leaves a young member of the staff to deal with some customers and promptly makes her way over to me. I had thrown on the first thing that I had put my hands on when I'd gotten out of the shower—leggings, my old running trainers, and a massively oversized football top that I usually wear only for bed. The poster had taken me by surprise and scared me. I need to find out where it came from. It must have been Ali. That's the reason she was at the holiday park tonight. But still, nothing is making any sense.

"Is everything okay?" asks Rose, meeting me in the centre of the lodge.

"Yes, yes." I manage to compose myself a little, aware that I must look and sound like a crazy woman to the other people here.

"I've, um, just found a message to me from an old friend. It was put under my door. I think it might have been left around the same time as the maid delivered some towels to my cabin. Would it be possible to speak to her just to see if she spoke to my friend or knows anything about it?"

"Yes, of course," replies Rose. She quickly crosses the room and picks up the intercom speaker asking for Claudia to come straight to reception.

A couple of minutes later, Claudia enters the lodge.

"You wanted to see me, Miss Donnelly?"

"Yes, thanks, Claudia. Miss Moore has received a note from a friend close to the time you dropped the towels in for her. Did you push a note under Miss Moore's cabin door or see anyone that did?"

I wait anxiously as Claudia retraces her steps from the previous hour at a painfully slow speed.

"I'm sorry, I definitely didn't leave a note. I don't remember seeing anybody else around when I dropped the towels in. I have only seen guests today."

I nod back at her, frustrated.

"Oh, but there was a lady who I saw a little earlier this evening," she adds suddenly. "I didn't recognise her. I assumed she was a new guest who hasn't been here before and was lost. She was coming out of the supply cupboard as I was going in. I thought she must have taken a wrong turn. It happens from time to time."

Rose starts to say something, but I rudely butt in.

"What did she look like?" I ask.

"I only saw her from behind. She was wearing a blue shirt, I think, with very long black hair," she answers, this time without hesitating.

My heart skips a beat. I nod silently and back away to the door. Claudia, Rose, the young guy on reception and their customers are looking at me confused.

"That's her, thank you Claudia." I manage to pat the girl affectionately on the arm as I pass before I leave the reception lodge. Once outside, I ram straight into the solid chest of a person standing in my path. I pause to try and pull myself together, and glance up at the man before quickly apologising. His hair is pulled into dreadlocks and he has bright green eyes. He accepts my apology before I rush past him.

*

I don't head back to my cabin. Instead, I make my way down to the beach. My head is spinning and I hope that some fresh air might start to help me see things a little more clearly. The stroll takes me less than ten minutes and I feel a small sense of relief as I slip off my trainers and let my feet sink into the cool sand. The sky is black and cloudy; the wind down here is strong and it whistles loudly in my ears. The shoreline is deserted and the rough sea beats against the shore in a soothing repetitive rhythm.

I walk farther away from the cabins leaving them behind me. I can hear the distant beat of music coming from the clubhouse accompanied by the sound of people cheering and clapping enjoying their summer holidays, like they should be. Tears threaten to fill my eyes and I wipe at my face angrily. Why is Ali doing this? She was fine to deliver the photo to the cabin today, so it seems she is in no danger. Why is she doing this to me? I feel as though I am part of a game that only she knows the rules to. *What does she want from me? Why is she trying to send me messages? Is it because she hates me because I unintentionally shunned her from my life when I met Jake? Will I ever know? Will I ever see her again?*

A gust of wind ruffles through my still-damp hair, causing an icy shiver to run down my back. I glance up from the sand. I'm standing near Logan's Tavern, which has closed for the night and sits shaded by the darkness of the pitch black beach. I slow as I get closer, where a silhouette I can't fully make out is loitering in the shadows watching me. The figure—a man maybe—is tall and well-built. He holds a cigarette in his hand, which he lowers to a table as his head snaps up and he seems to notice me looking at him. I wipe at the tears that have started streaming without warning down my face. Through my blurred vision, the man on the decking starts to become more clear. I let out a small sob, my knees going weak as I realise who the figure is. Jake.

I'm crying loudly now, unable to control it. Feeling as though I'm losing control, I turn quickly as he hears me and starts to head in my direction. Turning my back on the man I once loved, I start to run. But the sand is too soft and slows me too much. He soon reaches me and I hear him behind me. *Why was I so stupid? Why did I come back here?* My breathing quickens as he nears me. My heart hammers in my chest, making me dizzy.

I hit the rocks before I know it. I've stupidly run too far and gone past the steps that take me back to Ceaders. The rocks are slippery under my feet from the earlier high tide. My lapse in concentration does me no favors as my bare foot catches on a clump of seaweed and I slip, throwing me forward. I fall onto my knees and let out a yelp as the jagged edge of a rock slashes straight through my thin leggings, stabbing painfully into my shin. I bite my lip to stop myself from yelling out in sheer agony.

I listen as he gets closer; spray from the raging sea close to me covers my clothes. I'm frozen to the spot, still on my knees. I look around for an escape, and begin to scramble around on the rocks, but I know I won't be quick enough. I close my eyes and pray he hasn't seen me, that somehow and I can hide within the darkness or that I'm imagining it—like the other times in the past when I've mistaken another man for him. Through the foggy haze of confusion, fear, and pain, I hear a sound, a man's voice talking, but it's not one I recognise. Relief washes over me. It's not Jake.

"Are you alright down there?"

The man reaches me. A hand touches me lightly on the shoulder, causing me to flinch.

"It's okay." The man removes his hand from my shoulder and puts it in the air. "I'm not going to hurt you."

Slowly, I look up toward the figure standing above me. He puts out a hand and helps me to my feet leading me off the rocks and back onto the soft sand. My leg hurts like hell, and the dim light shows a shimmer of blood heavily patching my trousers. I wince as the salt from the rocks hits the fresh wound.

"Looks like a nasty cut," says the stranger, nodding down at my leg. Only when I fully look at him and come back to my senses, do I realise that he's not a stranger at all.

"Tom? Tom Logan?" I ask timidly, my voice quivers.

"Do I know you?" he asks, confused.

I nod, as he takes a step closer to me. He hasn't changed too much from how I remember him. The same dark hair and broad shoulders like Mark and the same big dark eyes. Though, he is much taller and clearly in a little better shape than his older brother.

"You, you used to," I stammer and try to force a smile, however, I don't think it radiates to my lips. "Emily Moore," I whisper, when he still don't click, still looking down at the ground. Embarrassed, I continue, "You probably don't remember me, I…"

"Of course I do," says Tom warmly, moving so that he is now positioned directly in front of me. "Mark mentioned you were back in town."

I take a cautious step backwards away from him to bring my feet onto the drier sand to stable my shakiness, but it doesn't work, I lose my balance again and stumble backwards clumsily.

Tom grabs my arm before I fall again.

"Come on, let's get you inside, you need to get that leg seen to."

I hesitate, but as I look back up to the cabins now far off in the distance I know that I won't be able to make it back up there without getting my leg strapped up first. I nod and take his arm as he wraps it around my waist and leads me to the tavern. He's holding a small burnt out tea light candle in his other hand, which I now see is what I mistook for a cigarette earlier. He follows my gaze.

"I was just busy clearing up for the night," he says, pushing the candle into the pocket of his jeans. "I heard you crying then saw you turn and start to run. I had to make sure you were okay. You look like you had seen a ghost."

"I thought you were someone else," I reply, quietly.

Tom doesn't question my despair, which I now feel wholly ridiculous for. He silently leads me up the steps and opens the door to the tavern for me as I limp through.

"Take a seat," he says. "I'll just get the first aid box." I hobble to the nearest booth and wince as I sit down.

"Everything alright, Tom?" asks a female voice that I can vaguely identify as the waitress who served me breakfast earlier today.

"Yeah, fine Tia, get yourself off home. I'll finish up here," replies Tom. His voice has hardly changed, still deep and husky like I remember.

The waitress bids him goodbye as she passes me and gives me a warm smile before heading out of the door and down onto the beach.

I glance around the tavern while I wait for Tom. It looks better at night than it did in the day. The bar in the centre is lit up and the tiny fairy lights woven through the fishermen's nets are now alight. Candles in glass holders dot each table and music plays quietly in the background.

"Got it!" says Tom, as he returns to my side with a green plastic box.

"Let's take a look at how bad it is." Gently, he rolls up my trouser leg. His touch is warm against my freezing skin. I barely notice the pain as his fingertips round the back of my leg and trace my calf, pulling the wound closer for him to inspect.

"Is it bad?" I ask, peeking only quickly at the blood-smeared area. The sight of blood has never agreed with me and I already feel sick to the stomach as it is.

Tom shakes his head. "Nah, just a nasty cut, it won't need stitches." He flashes a smile. "I think you'll live."

I manage a wry smile back, but still, I can't look Tom in the eye. I briefly wonder if it's because of the shock from believing he was Jake a few moments ago or maybe fear that my affection towards him all those years ago will come flooding back.

We stay silent as he cleans the wound and wraps it in a bandage. Tom eventually breaks the silence, and I finally bring myself to look him in the eye.

"You've changed since I saw you last," he says quietly, still crouched in front of me, now rolling down the tight material over my neatly bandaged leg.

"Really?" I ask. I suddenly become very aware of my appearance. My blood-soaked sandy leggings and oversized football shirt. My tear streaked face and now almost dry, windswept frizz of hair. I picture myself as I was when I left. The last time I saw him I was stick thin and had waist-length light hair. My hair colour has now darkened naturally over time and my figure is much curvier since the birth of Lucy. Under my clothes, my belly still bears the thin silver lines left behind by stretch marks. I had never lost the majority of the weight I had put on during my pregnancy with her and developed wide hips, a now moderate sized backside and larger breasts that I had never possessed back then. I look down self-consciously and cross my arms over my stomach area. When I look back up at Tom, he is staring at me intensely.

"You a football supporter?"

"Sorry?"

He nods to the football strip I have on.

"Oh, no, not really." I don't tell him it's a hand-me-down from my daughter's vast array of football gear. She took to following the sport from being small and has supported her home city ever since, something I have always found a little strange considering I have no interest and she has never had the influence of a father figure in her life.

Tom looks a little confused. "So you live up north now?"

I nod, not wanting to discuss it further. He notices my unease.

"All done." he says, quickly moving away from me, clearing the first aid supplies and rising to his feet.

"Thank you," I say sincerely, "and I'm sorry about before."

"No problem as long as you're okay."

I nod, "I'm fine. I should get going." I move, attempting to get to my feet but once again go dizzy and stagger back into the booth.

"Whoa." Tom moves back to help sit me upright. My face brushes across his cheek, rough from stubble as I bend my head forwards and bury it in my hands.

"Take your time, I've got nowhere I need to be." He moves back away from me towards the bar. "I'll get you a drink. You look like you could do with it. It'll calm your nerves."

He returns from the bar with a whiskey and hands me the glass. I can't help but notice he is left-handed and that he doesn't wear a wedding ring. I'm shocked. As he pulls his hand away, I catch a glimpse of a white scar on his wrist. It had been made by a close encounter with a Bunsen burner in the science lab at school—I had been the first one to see he had hurt himself and rushed over to help him rinse it under a cold tap.

I take the tumbler from him and sip the drink. It tastes disgusting and doesn't come anywhere near to calming me down.

"I thought you'd be married by now," I blurt out after draining the remainder of the whiskey and resting the cold glass against my now scalding forehead.

Tom smiles. "Nope. Not even close." He pours himself a small scotch, before refilling my glass, then pulls up a stool at the bar opposite me and climbs onto it. I throw back the second whiskey, now firmly in the sort of mood to get hammered.

"I'm sorry to hear about Ali," says Tom. "Mark said you had come back to try and help with the investigation."

"Yeah, me too," I reply, trying to push the image of the photo back at the cabin to the outskirts of my mind, for now.

"She used to be a great girl, although I haven't seen her in a very long time," he says, looking out of the window to the beach. The moon casts a white glow against the large waves, which are increasing in height.

"I'm sure they'll find her, Em."

I nod, tears filling my eyes again.

"Come on. It's getting late, let's get you home." He moves from the stool and helps me to my feet. "You're staying up at Ceaders, yeah?"

"Yes, but don't worry, I can manage—"

"No, you can't, I'll walk you back up."

I nod gratefully. Even though I assume Jake no longer lives in the area, the chance of bumping into him tonight suddenly seems very plausible.

Tom puts a jacket around my shoulders and locks up before we leave the bar behind. I pull it tight around my neck, nuzzling into the warm lining, searching for a sense of security I feel I need. I can smell his aftershave against the fabric every time the sea breeze brushes through it. I quietly inhale and lock the scent into my mind.

The walk back to Ceaders cabins takes three times as long as it had taken to get down to the beach and I now regret not going directly back to cabin after talking to Rose and Claudia. Tom leaves me at the steps to my cabin and waves as I unlock the door and let myself inside. The stifling heat hits me as soon as I am in, but tonight instead of it causing me to be uncomfortable, it feels welcoming and safe. I head straight to bed, emotionally exhausted from the events of the last twenty-four hours and it doesn't take long for me to pass out and enter another restless night.

Chapter 14

Well, well Emily what a mess you got yourself into tonight!

I watched, as you strolled along the beach, bathed in moonlight. God, even dressed in an old ratty football shirt you still looked gorgeous, but then you always did look good, no matter what you wore.

I nearly came to see if you were alright when I saw you fall, but then I knew you would be, you are stronger than you know. For that I admire you.

Once again, you didn't see me watching you from the shadows, perched on the cliffs above the bay. You really need to take in your surroundings more, Emily. You miss so much walking around with your head bowed to the ground the way you do. I really wasn't very far away at all. In fact, at one point you looked up from the rocks when you fell and I thought for a brief moment that you had seen me. But you hadn't.

I watched you as you left the tavern and walked back to the cabin with Tom Logan. What a handsome man he has turned into, hasn't he? Then, he was never exactly ugly even as a teenager. I even watched through the window as you got changed for bed. Your shoulders are a little burnt from the strength of the sun, you really need to take more care.

I waited until you fell asleep knowing that you were safe. I hope you sleep well tonight Emily, because I need you here as long as you can be and I don't want you tired. I'll be in touch, please be careful.

See you soon.

Chapter 15

The following day I wake with a tight knot buried in the pit of my stomach. Guilt, anxiety, fear; I'm not sure what I'm feeling. I know what I have to do today and it's going to be hard, but I can't face this alone anymore and I am utterly confused by Ali's actions from the past couple of days. I've hesitantly decided to give up trying to figure this out alone. I know I am taking a huge risk going against Ali's request not to involve the police but I can't do this on my own, I need help. Mark picks up his mobile on the second ring.

"Hi Em, what's up?"

"Mark, hi, erm, I need to speak to you. Are you free at any point this morning?"

"Yeah, of course. I'm heading to Cranley a little later, but I should be around till midday. If I'm not, then Chrissy will be."

"I'd rather talk to you… if that's okay?"

"Aren't you heading back home today?"

"Not till later on. So, is it okay if I pop into the station?"

"Yeah, sure. You alright, Em? You sound a bit upset."

I take a deep breath to steady my shaking voice. "Yeah, I'm fine. I'll be there in half an hour." I hang up on Mark and drag myself out of bed. Pain shoots up my injured leg and my whole body aches from head to toe.

In the bathroom, I splash water on my face and try to avoid my reflection in the mirror above the sink, where I know puffy eyes and dark circles will greet me. I can't shake the image of Jake from my head. Even though it wasn't even him I saw last night, it made me anxious and I know I need to get out of Sandbroke as soon as I can. Ali was at the holiday park yesterday, that's obvious. She's not hurt and she's certainly not dead, but she is trying to send me a message which I clearly am not clever enough to figure out. That's why I need to hand it over to the police, which I should have done from the start.

The sky is grey as I leave the holiday park and make my way as fast as my leg will allow to the main high street. I hope Mark hasn't been called away, although I know he will be furious that I kept information about Ali from him I know he will understand and at least I'm coming clean and telling the truth now. I was foolish to go against my instincts and lie. I know that now.

Rain starts to fall heavily and the wind increases tenfold in its strength once again as I near the street where the station is located. The sky instantly turns black as the forecasted storm makes its way obstinately towards Sandbroke. I didn't bring an umbrella and curse myself as the rain quickly soaks through the thin fabric of the cardigan I have on. The street soon becomes completely deserted. The few people who have braved today's weather run into a nearby café to take cover from the downpour or rush to head home and batten down the hatches until the storm passes.

I pick up my pace and try to jog, but pain shoots up from my shin so I am forced once again to slow my tempo. I look both ways before stepping out onto the road to cross to the station, that's how I don't know how I don't see it coming. Maybe because it is going so fast.

Out of my peripheral vision, I see a flash of colour—red, I think—and small, I'm not sure of the model, possibly a Mini. I don't even get the chance to fully look at the car before it rounds the corner and swerves onto the wrong side of the road heading towards me. I manage to take a small step backwards, avoiding the full collision. As the car's bonnet clips me, I feel myself flying into the air and back toward the pavement that I have just left. Through my blurred vision and the sheets of now suddenly torrential rain, I see the car speed off as an approaching police car pulls up near me and a woman gets out and runs towards me.

"Emily, Emily, can you hear me?" a voice I recognise but can't place asks. I try to nod my head, but I'm not sure if the thought has successfully made it into an action. Everything becomes fuzzy as voices slowly fade into the background before disappearing completely.

Chapter 16

Lightning strikes, brightly illuminating the small room I am in. Rain continues to pour down outside the window in never-ending transparent sheets. The sky is still pitch black, even though it's only just gone lunch time, and the wind is howling loudly adding to the drama of the storm that has now brewed to full strength overhead. A doctor takes my blood pressure and shines a small light to check my eyes, for what has to be the tenth time in two hours. I'm growing aggravated now. I've insisted that I'm fine, but they are keeping me in hospital for observation just to be sure.

Chrissy called an ambulance as soon as she found me on the side of the road. I had blacked out, but only for a few minutes and the doctors think that was just from the pure shock of what had happened. The accident keeps coming back to me in small flashbacks, but everything happened so quickly it is almost impossible to put the pieces together. Sharp pains shoot behind my eyes, another side effect of shock, so I'm told. I am in a state of confusion, but one thing I know for sure, what just happened to me was no accident, the driver didn't stop and the car sped off. I'm struggling to understand why I was the victim of a hit and run.

"Hi, Em," says Mark, as he rounds the corner of the A&E unit of Sandbroke General carrying two cups of coffee in a cardboard takeout holder, a concerned look on his face.

"Hi Mark," I say, propping up the pillows behind me to sit more upright, as I take one of the cups from him and briefly smile as I see Logan's Tavern's name emblazed in bright lettering on the side of the container.

"Tom says he hopes you are doing okay." Mark grins, when he catches me looking at the logo. I feel myself flush.

"They said when you can get out yet?" he asks. He carefully removes the plastic lid on his cup and gives his drink a quick stir. I notice he has dark circles under his eyes and that he looks in desperate need of a good night's sleep. I suppose just one of the many results of working as a as a chief inspector; you sign up to the stress the day you accept the badge.

"No, not yet," I answer. "My blood pressure has come down and they can't find any injuries apart from my leg, which happened before the accident. Apart from a little bump to the head and some bruises, I'm fine."

"You're one lucky woman," says Mark, as he sits down on the bottom of my bed and takes a sip of coffee. I bite my lip and look out of the window.

"I know." *If only he knew.*

"So, can you trace the car's registration?" I ask, hopeful.

"No, we've already looked, but the CCTV outside the station wasn't working."

"Why am I not surprised?"

"I know, the station is due to be revamped in the autumn. Unfortunately the CCTV is in the plans to get replaced. The system is probably almost as old as you are. Plus, it was knocked out of position by the wind from the storm."

I remain silent and nod. "Did nobody see what happened?"

"There was nobody around. The car had sped off by the time Chrissy got there."

"Is Chrissy still here?" I ask. She had brought me here and ensured I was attended to. But I hadn't spoken to her properly yet.

"Just passed her as I came in. She's on her way back to the station. She's adamant she's going to find the driver, but I think she's wasting her time. Just stupid kids passing through. The car is more than likely stolen. No doubt we'll find it abandoned somewhere along the coast."

"Will you thank her for me, when you see her?"

"Of course."

Mark shifts his weight on the bottom of my bed and takes a quick look at his mobile before returning it to his pocket.

"You should get going," I say, feeling guilty for taking him away from his work.

"Don't be stupid. So, what was it you wanted to tell me?"

"Pardon?" Caught off guard, I pretend I didn't hear him to give me a little more time.

"You were coming to the station to see me about something before the accident. What was it you wanted to talk about?"

I rub my aching head. Do I tell him? After all, that is what I was intending to do before someone rammed me with a car and could have easily left me for dead. I can't dismiss the sickening feeling it was some sort of warning. I was steps away from telling the police about Ali when it happened.

Thunder claps outside, sending a loud rumble through the room and causing me to shudder. I stay silent, then shake my head. "It was nothing important," I say.

Mark looks skeptical, but doesn't push for an explanation, though I know it won't be the last time he asks me about it. He is too good at his job to be unable to spot a bare faced lie when he hears one.

*

An hour later, I am discharged from hospital under strict instructions from the doctors to take it easy. Mark drapes a jacket around my shoulders once outside, the exact same thing his brother had done before walking me back to the cabin last night. Both men had clearly been brought up well and it feels reassuring to see that some chivalry still exists in the world, though it doesn't go far enough to fully restore my faith in the male species.

The rain is still heavy so I wait under cover for Mark to bring the car around to me. He takes me back to the cabin and sees me inside to get me settled for the night. I always thought of Mark as an older brother when he and Trish were together, and although her husband Max is a great guy, I still feel a little disappointed that it wasn't Mark she married. He has slipped straight back into the role he had years ago as an older protective brother-type figure to me, just like no time has gone by at all. He is a kind-hearted and genuine man, as he always was then, too. His wife is a lucky woman.

"Make sure you take a couple of days before you head back home, Em, a long journey on a packed train is the last thing you need right now," says Mark, before he climbs back in the car and starts the ignition. Unenthusiastically, I agree with him, although I want nothing more than to be back home in the comfort of my family.

Once inside the cabin, I lock the door ensuring that all bolts are fully secured when Mark leaves. I've not felt the need to use the extra security measure before now. But today, I feel on edge and suddenly very scared. Something feels different about the cabin, but I can't put my finger on what it is and dismiss the feeling almost instantly. Probably just because I have been cooped up in the hospital all day.

I call Lucy and speak to Mum and Dad in hope that their voices will lift my spirits. I don't tell them the events of my day, carefully sugar coating everything I do say to protect them. If I told them the truth, they would be on the first train down here tomorrow, and I don't want that.

I change into a pair of pyjamas and close all the curtains, shutting out the storm which is still going strong. I light the fire, feeling cold for the first time since I arrived back in Sandbroke, then I settle in front of the television and curl onto the couch. Throwing back a couple of painkillers that the hospital doctor prescribed me, I lie down. Thoughts of the accident play through my mind as they have done all day. I don't want to sleep. I don't want to be alone. I no longer feel safe.

The TV's noise fades as the storm rages on, thunder sounds and lightning illuminates the room in near succession as I let my eyes close. I count the number of seconds between each rumble and lightning strike, a trick my dad taught me when I was younger to measure how far off in the distance the storm actually is, usually miles away. I've never been fully convinced that this is an accurate measure and have settled on the more plausible explanation that it was possibly just a deterrent from my fear of storms as a kid. I can hear water dripping outside the window, *drip, drip, drip. A*t first it's irritating, but then the gentle rhythm starts to soothe me like that of a ticking clock. When pure exhaustion finally takes over and the pain starts to dull, I enter willingly into my subconscious.

At first, I dream of home. Me and my daughter in the park near our house on a bright autumn day, laughing and dancing, our feet crunching in the dry leaves that scatter the ground. Her long blonde hair catches in the low sun's rays and seems to sparkle like glitter, her skin pale and flawless, her cheeks rosy. Her pretty, big, blue eyes are full of happiness and hope for a future she is to enter; an endless array of possibilities and dreams stretched out in front of her, awaiting for her grasp.

But the dream soon changes. The bright colours begin to fade as black storm clouds emerge in the sky above us. I look up at them as they move closer and the air grows heavy and thick. Rain starts to fall turning the pretty park into a flooded mess of dirt and sludge. When I look to my side, Lucy isn't with me anymore.

The park has now disappeared, I am back in front of the police station standing exactly where I was this morning. Frightened, I try to wake up, but my exhaustion only leads to a deeper state of unconsciousness. I can see myself from above as the events unfold just as quickly as they did today; a blur of bright red bodywork, tinted windows and speed, the pungent smell of heated rubber and exhaust fumes.

Rain bounces hard off the already waterlogged road. The car gets closer, but this time its speed slows, enabling me to see inside it. I can make out the driver now. At first, it's not clear and I struggle to focus my vision. Tossing and turning, I fall even deeper into sleep, dreams now envelop me in a thick haze, leaving me paralyzed completely.

As the vision clears and the haze finally lifts, I can clearly see the driver of the car. The person is someone familiar. I can't yet place them, but I know it is someone from my past. Someone I think I once knew.

Chapter 17

A loud knocking wakes me from my slumber. My dreams quickly diminish with the morning light as I open my eyes and struggle to take in my surroundings, but then I realise I'm in the cabin and like a swift punch to the gut, the trauma of yesterday's events hits me full force. I limp to the front door. My leg aches and my neck feels stiff from a full night of sleeping on the small uncomfortable sofa. The room is stiflingly hot. The open fire has now burnt out. The whole area smells of burning wood and smoke.

"Who is it?" I shout through the solid wooden door so that my visitor can hear me clearly. I have no intention of opening it until I know who is there. My voice is croaky, my heart is leaping in my chest at the thought of who could be on the other side. *Ali?*

"It's only me," answers a slightly broken English accent that I immediately identify as Claudia's.

"Hi Claudia," I say, as I open the door to her. It must be late morning. I haven't yet looked at the time, but I know she doesn't normally start her cleaning round until around eleven.

"Hi, Miss Moore," Claudia says, beaming. "Rose asked me to bring these to you. We heard about your accident yesterday and would just like to say get well soon." She hands me a huge box of chocolates tied with a yellow bow.

"Oh, thank you, Claudia." I glance down at the luxurious looking truffles, my stomach churning in silent disapproval. "There is no need, really, I'm fine." I smile, wondering who it really is that I'm trying to convince.

"Oh, these were left for you too." Claudia reaches down into the hidden part of her cleaning trolley and produces a bouquet of flowers adding, "The gentleman didn't want to disturb you."

I take the flowers and thank Claudia again before she turns to leave. The card attached to the flowers is pink to match the beautiful arrangement that has been sent. At first I assume that they are from Mark or maybe Chrissy. Then have a sickening feeling that they could be from Ali, another clue to lead me to another dead end perhaps. But the flowers aren't from any of these people.

Emily,
Mark told me about the accident, hope you are doing ok.
Get well soon,
Tom xxx

I can't resist smiling at Tom's thoughtfulness. He hadn't seen me for years until my little stunt yesterday. I'm surprised it didn't leave him running for the hills. I must have looked like a mad woman. I place the flowers in a glass vase and pop them onto the window sill before getting dressed. I try to push the memories of the past couple of days to the back of my head as I leave the cabin and head down to Ceaders Bay.

The beach has a strange feel about it today. It is a lot cooler than yesterday and a dense fog floats on the sea's surface. The sky is gloomy and there seems a silent calmness after yesterday's storms. My leg still hurts as I put weight on it, but other than that, I feel much better than yesterday. I pause a for a few minutes, wrapping my arms around myself and look out over to the ocean, feeling lucky that I didn't sustain any more serious injuries and even more for the fact I am still alive. A few split second's difference yesterday, and it may have been a different outcome.

*

Tom is behind the bar as I enter Logan's Tavern. The place is relatively busy considering it is an overcast day. He nods to acknowledge me as I enter and finishes serving two elderly woman coffee and cakes before slinging a tea towel over his shoulder and turning his attention to me.

"Here's the wounded soldier," he announces, joining me at the end of the bar. "How you feeling?"

"Probably better than I should be," I admit truthfully. I feel the same warmth growing on my cheeks as I've always had in his presence.

"I just came down to say thank you for the flowers, they are beautiful."

"No problem," answers Tom, "I thought they might cheer you up."

I smile.

"Can I get you anything?" he asks. Moving away from me, he starts to wipe down the already gleaming bar area. I tap my fingers and purse my lips, deciding.

"Erm, yes, I'll have a coffee and one of those blueberry muffins please." I point to a pile of muffins in a display cabinet. I need to appear normal even if I feel anything but.

"Good choice. Coming right up." Tom smiles and heads off to the coffee machine at the other side of the bar as I pull up a stool.

I watch Tom contently as he works, seamlessly flowing from person to person, serving customers and chatting casually. Everyone appears to know him, even those who probably don't. They seem to gravitate towards him, to want a little piece of him. All the men want to be his friend and all the women want to be in his bed. Nothing has really changed in fifteen years, and sitting here now it's obvious to see why I never really stood a chance.

"So they found out who it was that almost ran you over?" asks Tom, joining me again at the end of the bar, only half joking.

"Nope, Mark thinks it was probably just kids, he says there's been a few cases of reckless driving in the town lately." I try to sound convincing as though I believe this too. Maybe I'm just being pessimistic; let's face it optimism has never come easy to me, so it wouldn't be the first time. Maybe

Mark's right and it really was just kids joy riding. A simple case of me being in the wrong place at the wrong time.

Tom nods, and slides a plate with a muffin in my direction. "You were lucky though, it could have been a lot worse."

"Yeah, I know." The same nervous feeling hits the pit of my stomach as I have had since I returned to Sandbroke. I take a small bite, then I push the barely touched muffin to one side.

"When are you heading back home?"

"I'm going to give it a couple of days. The doctor says just to take it easy for a little bit before travelling."

"That's good." I detect a look on Tom's face that suggests he is pleased I am sticking around for a bit, but I tell myself I have it wrong. I'm sure I am nothing but a tiny blip on his radar, just as I always was.

"Any news on Ali?" he asks.

"No, nothing. Mark mentioned they are considering broadening the search for her, which has to be a good thing. Right?" *She can't run forever.*

"I'm sure she's fine Em." Tom leans across the bar and rubs my hand affectionately.

"As far as I remember, Ali was a tough nut to crack. Anything that comes her way she will not back down easily."

Tom is right. Ali was always a fighter, she wouldn't back down to anything unless she knew she had given it her all, which is why I find it increasingly hard to believe she had ended up living the type of life she did; miserable, uneventful and from what I can gather living as a self-confessed social recluse.

"So… do you fancy joining me for dinner before you head back home?" asks Tom, taking me by surprise. I almost fall off my stool.

"Excuse me?" I gulp down the coffee that is suddenly wedged in my throat. Surely I misheard him.

"Dinner? It would be nice to catch up." Tom flashes me yet another knee weakening smile.

"I don't know, Tom. I…" I search for an excuse, but can't find one. It seems insane that I would decline the one man I had never really gotten over, but things are so different now, my life has moved on, and Jake has made it impossible for me to let anyone else in.

Tom seems to tap into my thoughts, lowering his tone he moves closer to me. "I'm not asking for your hand in marriage, Emily, purely platonic, I promise."

"Okay then." I cave sooner than I anticipated. "How about tonight?"

"You sure you feel up to it?"

"I think so."

"Great, tonight it is."

*

I'm not too sure I'm thinking straight as I head back up to the cabin. Maybe it's a mixture of delight at the thought of spending time with Tom and the strong painkillers pumping through my veins. Instead of making my way to the holiday park, I walk straight past it and head to the bus stop. I only have to wait for five minutes before the next bus to Cranley arrives. There's something niggling at the back of my mind. Something pulling me back to Ali's home and I hope to hell that it is something that is going to shine some light on her disappearance.

The journey takes longer than it did the other night. The bus is packed full of holiday makers unsure of what to do on a miserable day in a beach resort. Most of them get off the bus a couple of stops before me at a well-known indoor shopping outlet.

Ali's street looks different today; no longer glorified by an immaculate sunset and gleaming water as it was two days ago, it almost passes as ordinary.

It has started to rain now. Sand-filled puddles emerge on the pathways and leaves scatter the road left behind by wind damage from yesterday's storms. The beach is almost deserted today apart from the odd dog walker proving his or her dedication to the animal's well-being.

I am much more careful today when I enter Ali's house. The street is quiet, just as it was when I was here the night before last, but I don't have the cover of twilight to help me out this time. Again, there is nobody around. I know that Mark and Chrissy were heading up the team's search expansion today, so I hope that it will stay that way.

The house is dark inside; shadows dance on the gleaming marble floors as I make my way through. It feels as cold and uninviting as it did on my first visit. Outside the waves are now high, the ocean swirling deep and murky.

Once again, nothing is out of place and I doubt the police have been back yet. I pull out from my pocket a pair of rubber gloves, taken from one of the cabin's kitchen cupboards. I'm not going to make the same mistake I made last night by not covering my hands. If I do find anything, I want no trace of my fingerprints in this house.

I make my way through the rooms just as I had done last time. I don't know what I'm looking for, but I have a feeling the note behind the photo that I found was only one of the things Ali had left me. There has to be more. I have to be missing something.

Quickly, I make my way back up the stairs and towards Ali's bedroom. If there is anything else she wants me to find, it's going to be in that room. Inside, the air feels stale, the byproduct of almost two weeks of stifling summer heat and no ventilation. It's so warm it makes me sticky and uncomfortable. *There has to be something.*

I begin to hurriedly move around the room, a feeling of desperation building anxiously inside of me. I'm looking through drawers, cupboards, cabinets. But find nothing other than expensive looking items of jewellery and designer silk underwear. Some of the items appear brand new and I find it hard to believe that any woman would buy some of the skimpy and sexy garments she has without a man in their life to impress.

As I pull open the last drawer, losing hope once again, I notice something; a piece of fabric from one of the items is stuck in a gap in the drawer that seems out of place somehow. I roll up the sleeves of my jacket and reach as far back as I can to pull on the back of the drawer, It comes off easily. I stretch further until my arm burns from reaching up into the tight space behind the other drawers. My fingers hit against something small and I pull it out to reveal a plastic case. In it is a computer memory stick. I knew I was right to follow my instincts and come back to Ali's house. Hopefully, this small device will hold information for me to help her. It has to be pretty important. I feel a small but significant sense of hope, and for the first time since arriving here genuinely feel I am making some sort of progress amongst all the nonsense surrounding me.

I put the memory stick in my pocket and make my way outside, but as I am heading back downstairs I hear a sound and the front door starts to open.

Chapter 18

I dart back into Ali's bedroom and frantically search for somewhere to hide. There's nowhere apart from the wardrobe, so I dash to it and climb inside. I slide the huge door closed just in time. Whoever is here has just come through the front door is making their way up the stairs and straight for Ali's bedroom. I can hear their footsteps against the marble floor as they approach. I shuffle further into the wardrobe, burying myself amongst Ali's belongings like they are a form of camouflage. I flinch as something soft brushes my cheek, and sliding it to one side, I realise it's a heavy fur coat. The scent of Ali's perfume lingers in its lining. A strong, sweet scent. As I hear the door to the bedroom start to open, I crouch down and pull the coat over me. My heart hammers in my chest. If this is the police, as it most likely is, they can't know I'm here. As the person makes their way inside, I wonder who it is—Mark maybe? He said he and Chrissy were in the area today. I now regret coming, I should have left it until tomorrow when I know the police aren't in the area. *Maybe it's not even the police. What if it's Ali?* I want to find out, but can't chance opening the wardrobe door to see.

I listen as the person starts to move around the room. Drawers open and close, I hear rustling as Ali's belongings are moved around. They are looking for something. I begin to get more nervous when they don't leave the room as quickly as I had hoped. *What if they decide to search the wardrobe?* But as a mobile phone rings and the person speaks to answer the call, I feel a small sense of relief. It's Chrissy.

"Hi. What is it," she asks. She sounds slightly irritated. "Yes, no problem I'm on my way now," she adds, in a thicker-than-usual Mancunian accent. I see a shadow cross the small opening at the bottom of the wardrobe door as she passes, then I listen as she makes her way back down the stairs. I let out the breath I've been holding and scramble out from under the heavy coat. I leave it five minutes after I hear the front door click shut before I make my way down the stairs too.

Back outside, I thank my lucky stars that I managed to hide long enough for Chrissy to be called away. If she had found me there's no doubt about it that I would have been in deep shit. I quickly walk away from Ali's house. The small memory stick still in my pocket is burning a hole. I don't waste any time in heading straight to the nearest Internet café on the corner of Cranley's high street, I had spotted while on the bus on the way here earlier.

I am greeted by a well-built young guy dressed in long Hawaiian print board shorts and flip flops. His piercing green eyes are striking against his deeply tanned skin and his long blonde hair is spun into loose dreadlocks. I feel like I know his face but from where I'm not sure. He smiles at me as I enter the small shop and make my way towards him at the counter. Cranley has always been popular with surfers, thanks to its perfect sea conditions here. I have no doubt that this man's spare time is vastly taken up by the sport.

"Hi there," he says, blatantly looking me up and down when I reach him. He gives a small nod followed by a cheeky wink as if to tell me I've achieved some sort pass mark on his shag-o-meter.

"I just need to use one of your computers," I say coldly, nodding to the line of half a dozen empty computers at the back of the café. I'm grateful that the place is empty apart from me. I have no idea what is on the memory stick, and can do without any nosey strangers seeing its contents when I have no idea myself.

"No problem. Take your pick. How long do you want?" he asks moving to a till.

"I'm not sure yet, maybe just half an hour, for now."

I hand the man some money and he logs onto one of the computers for me. I notice the tail of what appears to be a snake tattoo poking out from under the sleeve of his T-shirt as he moves away.

"Just give me a call if you want anything," he says politely. His manner seems to have warmed. Maybe he's realised when he has seen me up close that I'm almost old enough to be his mother.

The guy leaves me. I swiftly remove the memory stick from my pocket and plug it into a free USB port. I'm not very computer savvy, but lucky for me, I have a fifteen-year-old daughter at home who is and have picked up a few tips from watching her over the years. I look around me to check where the guy is and see he is standing at the door talking to a blonde-haired girl dressed in a wet suit, a bright pink surf board tucked under her arm. I struggle to appreciate the lure of the sea on such a horrible day. I suppose it's a form of addiction.

After the computer runs a security scan I promptly click on the memory stick's icon as soon as it loads onto the screen, wondering what could be so important that Ali would feel the need to hide it. Maybe it's something to do with her finances, bank details, tax information, or account spreadsheets. Owning a house like the one she has must warrant a lot of money and a lot of upkeep, I would presume.

There is only one file when the memory sticks contents open, a Microsoft Word document. I click on it and it immediately blinks onto the screen. It is obvious by reading the first couple of lines that this isn't financial. In fact, it's nothing to do with money whatsoever. It's a diary. It's Ali's diary. I smile, remembering back to how Ali had always kept a diary when she was a teenager. Back then, it was in the more favorable paper book and pen format. She hid that one, too, under a loose floorboard in her bedroom and only Jenna and I knew anything about it. By the looks of it, she only started writing this one six months ago. I can see already that it only goes back to January this year, not long after the date she returned to the area. I glance around to check the coast is still clear and click to print the document hoping that the printer I am connected to is nearby. I'm relieved when I hear a clicking in the corner furthest from where the guy stands and the diary is printed quickly for me to collect.

I grab the memory stick and bury the loose sheets of paper in my handbag before I rush back out of the door.

"You finished already?" asks the guy as the blonde girl he is with eyes me curiously.

"Yes, thanks for your help." I say, as I dash past them. "Anytime," he replies.

*

I make my way to the marina not far from where Ali lives. I know there isn't another bus to Sandbroke for almost an hour now and I can't wait that long to read what she has written, but I need to get further away from her house in case anyone sees me.

The sky is beginning to clear as I approach the once small marina. The strength of the sun now starting to come back to its full force, burning away what is left of the heavy clouds from earlier this morning. The marina was here when I was younger and I remember it pretty well from when Jenna, Ali, and I came here to visit the beach club on a Friday night. Back then it housed nothing more than a few old fishing boats that were no longer in use and the odd rundown wreck that was in the process of being restored to its former glory. Now, it seems to have doubled in size and houses glamourous looking boats and private yachts. The whole place is coated with a thick layer of wealth.

I walk around the marina until I find a seat that is situated in a corner away from the boarded jetty and the relatively busy area. Settling down, I reach inside my bag and pull out Ali's diary. I pull my sunglasses down over my eyes, take a deep breath and begin to read.

Part Four

Ali

Chapter 19

Winter in Cranley can be a peculiar time. Tourists that had graced us with their presence over the summer and into early autumn are now long gone, and with very little to now do, the locals take to part-time hibernation for the next few months.

I look out of the office window to the almost deserted streets below. The branches on the trees that line the pavements are stripped bare and I can't help but feel they look menacing under the low red sun that is setting far off in the west over the ocean, currently just out of view from where I sit. Dr Langley—or Monica, as she insists I call her—shifts her chair closer to me, and thoughtfully twiddles with an expensive-looking silver parker pen.

"I'll say it once and I'll say it again, Ali, your mother's death wasn't your fault," she says, in that mildly patronizing tone of voice she sometimes uses.

I manage a smile but really don't understand how she could possibly know what she is really talking about. Years of expensive education, a printed certificate—which she no doubt has framed somewhere in her Pemblington based home where she resides with her perfect husband and three beautiful children and a few additional letters at the end of her name—

doesn't make her a mind reader, nor does it enable her to glimpse into the past. If she could then she would see that she is wrong. I choose, as usual to ignore her.

"Did you know that the sun's rising and setting point changes slightly every day?" I hear myself ask. At least, I think it's me, it's hard to tell these days. Dr Langley doesn't respond, so I continue. "It moves south gradually, until it finally hits the winter solstice." I trace an arched circle in the air with my finger, invisibly mapping out the route that it takes.

Dr Langley sighs, and moves to pull down the blind at the window, blocking my view. She clearly is not impressed by my knowledge of the celestial body. I have no choice but to set my focus back on her.

"Your mother was very ill, Ali. How do you think it would make her feel to know that you are blaming yourself for something that was totally out of your control? God is the only one who has a say in who lives and dies on this earth."

Oh, here she goes again. Dr Langley cannot get through a full session without bringing God into the equation, she's simply incapable.

"Yeah, I know Monica." I'm telling her what she wants to hear. As I always do in our weekly sessions in hope that they will conclude more quickly, but somehow she sees through my lies. Maybe she does have mystical powers, maybe she is just damn good at her job. She starts to talk again, I lean back and look at the closed blind to the window, suddenly feeling claustrophobic. I shut my eyes.

*

A while before I discovered my mum had become sick, my life was pretty near perfect. I didn't have a husband or kids, but that's the way I wanted it. That's what I chose. I settled down in London. I loved it there; the hustle and bustle, the traffic, the noise, even the smog and its ridiculously busy roads and the overcrowded tubes found a place in my heart.

My career as an actress really took off in London. After acting in small television roles, I landed myself a fantastic job in a television crime drama series and although it wasn't a leading role it was still a good one. Some places I went people would even shout my screen name and ask me for photos and autographs. I'm not saying it was anywhere near the level of attention a Hollywood actress would get, but it was enough for me. The expensive drama school that my mum had scrimped and saved so hard for over the years to send me to had finally paid off and I had achieved what I had always wanted. My life was a whirlwind of social events, glamorous parties, and photo shoots. I travelled the world or pretty damn close, and lived a life of pure content. I bought an apartment with a partial view of the Thames and got carried away with my glamorous lifestyle.

I had lived in London for almost five years, before the show was suddenly cancelled and I was unexpectedly unemployed. After that, I managed to get work, but competition was fierce and my age was against me by then. It seemed that reality shows and scantily clad twenty-somethings willing to show their boobs at any given opportunity were the 'in' thing. Although I have never been the shy and retiring type, that wasn't for me. Work from then on mainly consisted of small supporting roles gained through contacts and old colleagues pulling strings within the industry, but it was nowhere near the level of work I had been used to. It didn't keep me busy enough. I became bored and soon started to miss home. My life itself became a lot less fast-paced and my social life basically nonexistent. It's amazing how many so-called friends, even those I thought I were close to slowly start to drop one by one when the fame begins to dry up.

When I received the news that my mum was in bad health, I came straight back home. I had managed to get back to Sandbroke to see her occasionally while I had been living in London, which admittedly wasn't enough. I was selfish and far too self-absorbed to find the time. Mum had never let on how sick she really was until near the end, but I was lucky enough to spend a short time with her before she passed. A little while later, she was gone and that's when I found myself totally alone and a new and very different life began for me.

"Ali, are you even listening to me?" my eyes snap open.

"Yes, yes, sorry Monica of course I am." I sit upright in my seat and try to show more interest.

"Have you been getting out and about more often like we discussed last time?" she asks me, the silver pen is poised ready to write down my every word when I answer. She clicks the top of it a few times and I fight the urge to rip it from her perfectly manicured fingers and throw it across the room.

"A little," I answer quietly.

"That's good, at least you are starting to leave the house now. It'll be good for you to get out and about more."

I raise my eyebrows and cock my head as if I'm interested. In fact, I'm trying my damnedest not to scowl at her. I was scolded like a child for not showing enough awareness last week, and I don't want these stupid therapy sessions to go on any longer than humanly possible.

"And what about the new house, have you settled in now?" she asks.

"Yes, just about." I smile as I think about my beautiful home by the sea. The one thing that keeps me close to sane these days.

"It's all furnished and decorated now. You will have to pop around for a coffee some time. I'll give you the grand tour." *Wow, that sounded pretty sincere. My acting skills certainly come in handy in these sessions.* In reality, I've done very little with the house since I moved in almost two months ago, and with the exception of my own bedroom haven't really touched any of the other rooms yet; they are still the same as the previous owners left them. Although I'd like to change them because they aren't at all to my taste, I haven't really had the willpower, desire, or even the energy to start redecorating just yet. Some days I find it a struggle to even get out of bed in the morning.

Monica sits forward and looks genuinely honored by the invitation to my house.

"Well, yes, Ali, I would love that."

Monica has wanted to befriend me since we met in my first session. She constantly compliments me on my clothes and my hair and makeup. At first, I thought the compliments were just to try and boost my now almost non-existent self-confidence. Now I see that it may be more of a small infatuation towards me, a bit of a girl crush on her part.

I smile agreeably and casually glance at the clock on the wall behind her. Five more minutes and I can get out of here. The only reason I come is because my GP pretty much told me I have to. After my mum died, I had a breakdown, and along with the antidepressants, this is meant to be a huge help when dealing with bereavement. I prefer the medicinal route by far.

"Have you made any friends in the area yet?" asks Monica. "Are you back in touch with any of your old friends?"

I shake my head. "No, I don't really know anyone in the area. Anyway, I'm originally from Sandbroke and I don't have a reason to go there anymore, now Mum has died."

Monica nods and glances down at the designer handbag I have on my lap. She has already commented that she likes it. She can have it for all I care. I wonder at what point in time I became so materialistic. The saying really is true; money can't buy you happiness. What it can do, however, is buy you lots of expensive and meaningless crap to help disguise how unhappy you actually are.

I plaster on the sickly sweet fake smile again and try to keep the conversation flowing.

"I've made a new friend in Cranley recently," I announce, enthusiastically.

"Oh, Ali that's wonderful news!"

"Yes, I know. Her name is Missie. We've spent quite a lot of time together recently."

"Really, and what is this Missie like?" she asks, her voice is monotone. I detect a slight look of jealously cross her face, which is soon replaced with a warm smile.

"Oh, she's lovely. We get on very well. We go walking most days," I reply.

Monica clearly doesn't even realise I'm totally taking the piss out of her. *Not that smart Dr lady, are you?*

Monica smiles again, then glances down at her watch and finally puts down her annoying pen.

"Okay, well, I think that's us for this week, Ali. But you know where I am if you need to give me a call, even if it's just for a chat." She rises to her feet and follows me to her office door to see me out.

"It seems you are making very good progress, Ali."

"Yes, I know. I think I'm getting there," I lie.

Chapter 20

I first saw him on a bitterly cold, clear January day. I was on the Pier in Cranley completing my daily walk with my neighbour—Mrs. Robertson's Springer Spaniel, Missie. She was running full pelt ahead of me, ears flapping in the breeze, her tail wagging in the delight at the thought of being free for the next couple of hours. She was soaked from an impromptu dip in the ocean and was overly eager to get back into the freezing cold water.

"You've got no chance, young lady," I shouted at her, as she neared the railings of the pier and began to whimper down at the sea.

"Wait till we get back to the beach, where the water is more shallow, girl." Missie seemed to understand what I had said and continued to bound on her quest towards the pier end. When she got there, she stopped abruptly at a random man, who bent down and began to stroke her.

I knew who he was as soon as I got closer to him and we made eye contact, how could I not? I'd had a bit of a crush on him when I was younger, but he was well and truly taken back then.

"Cute dog," he said, as Missie curled up at his feet and settled there like she had known him forever. They say that dogs are a good judge of character and I found myself wondering in that instant if that was really true.

"Yeah, she's not mine. I just walk her for a neighbour," I responded. I felt his eyes on me and instantly regretted not putting on any makeup before leaving the house. I picked up my pace, closing the small gap between us.

"I'm so sorry, she has you soaked." I pointed down at his trousers where a stain of sand and sea water crept up the bottom of his checked shirt and covered his crotch. My eyes lingered in the area longer than they should have. Realising what I was doing, I looked quickly away a little embarrassed.

"Do I know you?" he asked. Still staring. "You look very familiar."

"Yeah," I answered. "We knew each other when we were younger. I'm Alison, Ali Martin."

"That's right," he snapped his fingers in the air. "I knew I recognised your face. Long time no see." He shivered and moved his arms over his chest as a blast of icy cold air crossed the pier. "You look well, Ali."

I ignored his statement because I knew he was just being polite. To anyone with eyes in their head, I looked like crap.

"How have you been?" I asked him casually, pulling my scarf tighter around my neck as it tried to escape on the strengthening frozen breeze.

"Honestly… I've been better," he replied. At that moment I realised he looked a little sad, like he had the weight of the world perched on his shoulders. His eyes were still boring into me; sexy and seductive, like they always used to be.

I nodded "Yeah, me too." We stayed silent, just looking at each other. I searched for the words that old Ali would have chosen to use next in this sort of situation: 'Let's get you out of those wet clothes, that will cheer us up.' or 'I know a good way we can get warmed up together,' would have been up there. But new Ali settled on, "It's freezing, would you like to join me for a coffee?" I pointed to the marina perched in the distance near the end of Cranley beach. To my surprise, he accepted. And that's how it started.

*

Over the next few months, I opened up to him like I hadn't done with anyone in years, and he was there for me, listening. A shoulder to cry on and a mountain of support at the darkest time in my life to that point. It became an almost daily routine for me to meet him on the pier in Cranley, usually when I was walking Missie in the evenings. We spent hours talking, but we were careful not to discuss too much about the past, as both of us had been through some pretty bad times. We both wanted to forget it and move on.

Soon, the meetings turned into more than just a gentle stroll along the beach. We would spend time together wherever and whenever we could. Things moved fast between us, but neither of us made any attempt to slow down the pace at which our relationship was developing. I felt myself falling for him hard. There was a passion between us that I'm sure many would envy. Ultimately, we both just wanted the same thing—to be loved. On the two-month anniversary of us meeting at the pier end, he presented me with a gift, a beautiful delicate silver charm in the shape of a four leaf clover. Holding my hand in his, he attached it to the bracelet hanging on my wrist. He told me that I should wear it all of the time and it would bring luck my way. I told him that I had already used up my whole life's share of luck the day I found him.

Another month rolled by, and finally winter started to melt away to fuse into spring. My mood was the highest it had been for a very long time and I was the happiest I can ever remember being. Then, out of nowhere, on a chilly April night at the end of the pier in the exact spot it had all begun, he ended it. I didn't see it coming at all and was totally shocked and heartbroken. He told me he loved me, but things were moving too fast, he couldn't deal with the way he felt about me and the timing was all wrong. Through tears of rage, I ripped the charm from my bracelet and flung it at him. As he bent to pick it up from the wooden pier boards, he told me he wanted me to keep it. I told him my luck had just run out before I turned and left him standing at the pier end. That was over a month ago now; I haven't seen or heard from him since.

I went on a rapid downward spiral soon after he left me. I thought I'd found happiness and I thought that he felt the same, but now I see that was never the case. I often wonder if he was just using me as so many men have done in the past, happy to be seen with me on their arm, but not prepared to settle down, open their hearts, and spend the rest of their lives with me. I thought he was different, but I see now he wasn't.

I spent a lot of time alone living off takeaways and drinking away my sorrows. Life turned into one long monotonous circle each day, exactly the same as the last—Groundhog day at its precise definition. I hardly left the house, and the farthest I went was to the end of the pier and back with Missie, but even that became far less frequent. The pier brought back too many memories of him and I wanted nothing more than to permanently erase every memory that I had with his face in it.

The darkness in my head was back swirling in my mind like the sea outside the window of my home on a stormy night. I tried to battle against it, but it was no use. So instead, I stopped fighting and surrendered.

Chapter 21

On my darkest day, I found myself on an isolated Cranley beach in the middle of a freak spring storm. Hailstones lashed down bouncing off the sand and scattering messily across its wind-battered surface. I walked to the sea where the waves raged ferociously, melting into a clouded dark and moody sky. I didn't halt and kept walking until the water splashed over my shoes and bare ankles, then further until it was to my thighs. I winced as I waded out even further and the icy water circled my waist, piercing my skin and cutting deep into my bones. My clothes instantly started to get heavier as they became weighted down by sea water. The hailstones continued relentlessly, bouncing down into the ocean like bullets from gunfire in war. I wondered what it would be like—to let the water consume me, to succumb the icy lure and simply disappear. My thoughts flashed at one hundred miles per hour through my brain, but regardless of the temperature, I was already numb to any real emotion by that point.

Somewhere in the distance, I heard a voice over the noise of the sea. I looked behind me to see a man walking a large dog along the beach. He quickly let go of the dog's lead and ran towards me.

"Are you crazy? Get out of the water, lady," he shouted loudly over the sound of crashing waves. When he reached the sea, he kicked off his shoes and started to make his way in, beckoning me towards him when the sea finally reached his knees. His dog stood motionless at the water's edge barking loudly. As the man got closer, I studied him and saw he must only be young, maybe twenty or twenty-one at a push. His long hair was soaked from the weather. I backed up further until I was standing breathless, parallel to him. I didn't want him to be harmed and he was already in deep enough.

"Whoever he is, he's not worth it," he yelled, only half joking, as he waded out of the water and waited for me to follow him. It was as if he knew.

I backed up further until I was back on dry land and toppled as my legs finally gave way beneath me.

"You alright?" he asked, an air of genuine concern filled his voice and even in my distraught state I found myself quickly liking him. He ran over to me unzipping his coat at the same time. Kneeling by my side, he gently wrapped it around my shoulders.

I nodded gratefully. My teeth were chattering so much I was unable to talk. My whole body shook beyond my control, a firm warning of what must have been no more than thirty seconds in the sea in the middle of a storm can do to the human body.

"Do you live close?" the man asked. As he moved away, his shirt sleeve caught in the wind, showing a glimpse of an extremely well-detailed and realistic python tattoo on his upper arm.

I managed another nod and turned to point at my home, now directly behind us.

"Come on." He helped me up from the cold sand. "I'll walk you up."

We began the short walk to my house and the young man put out his hand. I shook it lightly, which resulted in pain shooting up my arm as it gradually began to thaw out under the strangers heavy coat.

"I'm Callum," he said. He appeared more confident than his years should allow.

"Ali," I replied. I recognised him but couldn't think where from.

Callum walked me to the gates of my house where he bid me farewell and told me to look after myself. By then, the storm had subsided and a small haze of weak sunshine was peeping through the increasing gaps in the clouds.

Callum and I had talked during the walk back up the beach to my house, well, I'm saying 'we.' Callum did most the talking whilst I listened. He told me that he was a keen surfer, and that he had recently finished studying IT at Uni and was now living in Cranley with his brother. He was currently looking for a job to earn some extra cash to enable him to get a place of his own. For now, he worked as a lifeguard on Cranley Beach during the summer season. I realised that is possibly where I recognised him from. I learned his girlfriend had recently dumped him for an older man and that his Doberman was called Rex named after one of his dad's favourite bands.

I felt downright stupid for what he had just witnessed me doing, but he made me feel comfortable and as the warmth once again came back to my limbs, the embarrassment had soon started to fade. Outside the gates of my house, I gave him back his coat and thanked him for his kindness. I told him I would buy him a coffee the next time I saw him on the beach. It was too little to thank him for what he had just done.

Back at home, I tried to put the afternoon to the back of my mind. I could still feel the sea as it sunk into my pores and froze me to the core, but it hadn't numbed the pain as I had wanted. I saw Callum's friendly green eyes and it reminded me that not everyone in this world is bad and that hope may be out there. I just had to be patient. I busied myself cleaning and organizing the house because I needed to do something to keep my mind focused.

Later, I settled down with a bottle of Merlot for company as darkness crept in and the night approached. I would be glad when the day was over. The sky outside was clear now and a strange calm had descended after the storm had passed.

When the second bottle of wine was half finished, I finally started to relax. I lay back on my beautiful sofa and glanced around my perfect room, absorbing my stunning view and hoping for an idyllic life. As I closed my eyes and the torture of the day finally faded away, I dreamt that someone was standing in the corner of the room with me. Hidden in the shadows. Watching me sleep.

Chapter 22

I watched you today as you walked along the pier, storm clouds gathering quickly in the distance. You look so sad, Ali. Is it hard to accept that the once famous and adored Alison Martin has turned into a nothing? They say what goes around comes around and in your case, it has. I watched as you walked along the pier, your long dark hair blowing behind you in the breeze. You cried at the pier end for the love you thought was forever. Nothing is forever, Ali, you of all people should know that.

I watched Missie curl into your arms like a baby as you held her and sobbed until there were no more tears left to cry.

Later, I watched you walk back to the beach and the storm touched down, and as the lure of the choppy waves beckoned you towards them. It's a real shame that a beauty such as yourself didn't end up with the beautiful life to match.

You didn't spot me on the beach as I watched as you walk into the ocean. I wondered what it is you were trying to do. Then I watched as you entered your mansion. I followed you in a little while later, using the key I keep in my pocket, that you don't know I have.

I was in the house with you for quite a while, not that you noticed. I hid in the shadows and watched as you cleaned the already immaculate rooms, furiously trying to banish the dark thoughts in your mind. I watched as you drank to forget and saw the tension in your shoulders start to disappear.

I watched as you passed out, your breathing soon became heavy and settled into a comfortable rhythm. While you were sleeping, I crept through your house, looked through your belongings and did what I came to do. You think it's getting better but the truth is, it will only get worse. Don't worry, Ali. Not long now.

See you soon.

Chapter 23

I suppose some would say that starting up a little charity work was the pivoting point in my life. Dr Langley—Monica—suggested that it might be a good idea to get involved with some of the hospital charity and fundraising events, so I did and the couple that I have been involved in up to now have been good.

My social life is also becoming a little better. I have made a friend. She has recently moved to Cranley and we have found we have quite a lot in common, have the same interests and have dealt with the same sorts of troubles in life. It's good to be wanted by people and to have someone to talk to. Although I'm still grieving over the loss of my mum and the break-up of my relationship, things are slowly beginning to get better. I'm starting to feel like me and I've even started my daily walk along the pier again.

I've been thinking a lot about Jenna and Emily lately, my friends from back at school. I wonder if I should contact them and hope that maybe I can trace them. I regret losing touch and could do with their friendship now. Maybe I'll try to get in touch with them soon.

I saw him yesterday. The man that recently broke my heart was at the hospital. I passed him in a waiting area after I'd finished my weekly appointment with Monica. He didn't see me or at least, I don't think he did. I wondered what he was there for then quickly reminded myself that his health is no longer my concern. But still, I kept thinking about him for the remainder of the day. I hope one day I will be able to stop caring for him and wonder if that place in time will ever come to me.

So my life continues, and admittedly day by day I get better and better. My doctor has reduced my medication dosage, and Monica even says that if my progress continues at the rate it is going I can stop with the sessions. But even they are far less tedious these days.

As the weeks pass, life has gone from pretty terrible to bordering on good. Finally, I can start to live again. There is only one flaw in my plans–something that I must report to the police, but have not yet had the evidence to take to them. It's happened before in the past, something that comes with the territory when you have been in the public eye, as I once was. It could even be in my head, my imagination playing games with me. It wouldn't be the first time. So I'll just leave it for now. I'll wait a little longer and see if the feeling passes.

The overwhelming feeling that almost every day, I am being watched.

Part Five
Emily

Chapter 24

There's a distinct chill in the evening air as I head along the beach to Logan's Tavern. Although I'm not too sure if the chill is formed from the weather itself, or it is inside me already, nestled deep in the marrow of my bones. Either way, it feels as if it's growing by the minute. Thoughts of Ali play out in my mind, her words in the diary and her overall state of mind as she described has shocked me, and I briefly wonder how much I really knew her at all.

I've read about how low she was and how a mysterious man she did not name lifted her from the deepest, darkest place she has ever been, only for him to callously throw her back into it a few months later. I wonder who he is, and why she didn't mention his name. Maybe the thought of writing it caused her even more unnecessary heartache. She was obviously trying hard to forget about him and cut the connection they had clearly shared in the beginning.

I read how she had contemplated suicide and would have possibly let herself drown if a young man named Callum hadn't intervened on the beach. I thank God that he showed up that day.

I've read about how a blossoming friendship and involvement in some charity work that she loved had given Ali a new lease of life and with it, the hopes of a new beginning. That's where the diary ended, bringing me up to date with her life since she returned, up to near the time she first contacted me. Love, loss, death, friendships, ups and downs—pretty standard for most normal lives, just to an extreme extent, spanned over the short space of six months for Ali.

As I continue along the beach, I try my best to attempt to put Ali's written words to the back of my mind. Mark and Chrissy say she will be fine and I must talk myself into believing they are right.

*

Tom and I had arranged to meet at his bar for a drink before we head for a pizza in the town centre. My stomach has successfully managed to twist itself into a hundred knots by the time I reach Logan's Tavern. I stop before I enter, nervously smoothing down my windswept hair over my shoulders and adjust the waistband of my jeans, pulling at them to rest on my hips. I catch a glimpse of myself in the glass doors and question why I am here. Although I have tried to make myself look half decent with a lick of makeup and a pretty lace top, still I wouldn't describe myself as anything other than borderline average.

Tom greets me as I enter. He's sitting at the same booth that we had been in when he tended to my wounded leg, I can still feel his fingers lingering on my skin, warm and soft, and a shiver of excitement runs through me as I sit down opposite him.

"Hi, Emily, you look great!" He stands as I near him.

"Thank you, so do you," I say casually, nodding towards his red-checked shirt and dark blue jeans. Let's face it, the guy could have shown up in a black plastic bin bag and I would have still swooned. I'm pretty sure he knows that.

"Take a seat." I sit down opposite him as directed before Tia—the waitress I saw here last night—appears next to me.

"Can I recommend the cocktails?" she asks, as she politely hands me a menu. "I make the best strawberry daiquiri on the coast, and don't let this one tell you any different." She points at Tom who starts to chuckle.

"Stop trying to impress the boss, Tia," he jokes. I scrutinize the menu and decide on a less potent concoction of exotic-sounding fruit juices mixed with vodka, but make a promise to Tia I will give the famous daiquiri a try another time. Tom orders a beer and the waitress promptly turns to leave us.

Tom laughs again as she goes and shrugs his shoulders, "What can I say, you can't get the staff these days."

"Don't knock it," I respond, "being a waitress is bloody hard work!"

"Oh, how do you know? Is that what you do now?" he asks, interested.

I nod, feeling a little embarrassed, though I'm not too sure why.

"I always thought you'd end up being an artist or a sculptor. If I remember rightly you were never away from the arts block at school. But then again, you were good in all subjects, you always were a bit of a swot," he says, as our drinks arrive.

"Apart from maths," I correct him. "Anyway, you can talk." I reach over the table push him playfully on the arm. "If *I* remember rightly, you came out of secondary school with the highest set of grades it had seen in years."

It was true. Tom had graduated high school with the highest grades available for all subjects in his final exams and set an all-time high for Sandbroke High. I remember thinking how unfair it was, that he was allowed to be so intelligent and have the level of popularity that he did too. Not only was being the most popular guy in school enough, but he also had the most beautiful girlfriend and he was the captain of the football team, which, of course, was at the top of its league. The cliché of the perfect catch that you see in all teenage chick flicks is alive and well, and is now sitting opposite me, drinking a bottle of Bud.

"How is Olivia?" I ask. The image of Tom's simply stunning high school girlfriend now rooted firmly in my head—perfect hair, perfect teeth, perfect figure and ultimately loved by all. I envied her growing up; she was everything I wanted to be and possessed everything I wanted to have back then. "Does she still live in Sandbroke?"

"She certainly does. Married, with four kids now," he adds, before taking a casual sip from his bottle. "She and Peter were married eight years ago."

"You mean Peter Morley…"

"Yep, Pete, you remember him! My best friend back then. He still is now, actually. I was his best man at their wedding."

I can't help but laugh out loud. Olivia used to dote on Tom, she followed him around like a sheep. They had still been together when I left Sandbroke, and I didn't think she would have ever let him go. "Wow, how times change," I announce, mockingly.

"Yes, they certainly do. Olivia and I were never really a good match. She and Pete are much better together." There's a pause, then Tom's eyes meet mine.

"So what about you, Emily Moore? Weren't you madly in love with Jake Saunders?"

I keep calm. Maybe the vodka is starting to work its magic because my heart hasn't started pumping nearly as quickly as it usually does at the mention of Jake's name.

I fiddle with the straw in my drink, unable to meet Tom's forceful stare.

"No, we split up a couple of years into the relationship."

"And then you moved to the North East?" I can see that Tom has put two and two together. It isn't hard. I don't try and deter him from working out my reason for leaving was Jake. I nod.

"And what about now?" he asks, his tone lowered. I detect a slight awkwardness to him that I've never seen before. "Are you seeing anyone?"

"No. No man in my life; carefree and single." *If only he knew.* I drain what is left in my drink and Tom promptly calls Tia over to get us another round.

"I'm surprised that you've not settled down, though," I say, when she leaves us again. Carefully maneuvering the conversation away from my non-existent love life.

"How do you mean?" he asks, sounding genuinely puzzled.

"Well, you had about fifty girls lining up back at school, you could have taken your pick." I use my fingers to begin to count. "There was Polly, Rebecca, Jayne, Victoria…" I begin to ramble, rattling off a list the girls who had admitted to having a thing for Tom back in school, before he puts up a hand to stop me. "They would have all jumped at the chance to go out with you."

Tom's eyes finally meet mine. "What about you?"

I almost choke on an ice cube. "What do you mean?"

"Would you have said yes, if I'd asked you out back then? If I got there before Jake?" Tom cocks his head and smiles, that confident smile that has no worries, self-assured and bordering cocky.

I flush. Suddenly, I'm fifteen again, standing at my locker in the school corridor as he goes past, surrounded by flocks of friends and female admirers, not even turning to give me a second glance, blissfully unaware of my existence. I summon some courage, God knows where it comes from; perhaps the vodka. I'm almost thirty-five years old; I'm not a kid anymore. He doesn't possess the same power he once had over me as a loved up teen. *Or at least that's what I'm telling myself at this moment in time.*

"You know I would have said yes," I say softly. "You didn't even notice me."

Tom leans closer to me across the table, but doesn't get the chance to reply as a different waitress comes over to our table and hands Tom the phone.

"It's Bill Collier, Tom, he wants to know something about the fresh seafood order you placed last week. Are you alright to talk to him?" she asks.

Bill Collier was a keen fisherman back when I lived here and was once a good friend of my dad's. I presume he must have gone on to cast his nets further afield now and sell his daily catch as a profession.

"Yes, I'll speak to him," Tom answers, before turning to me. "Sorry, Em."

"It's fine," I reply.

Tom sighs and rises to his feet. Taking the phone from the waitress, he moves away, motioning to me that he will be two minutes. I smile back, thankful for the interruption, to cool down, pull myself back together and get my head out of the clouds.

When Tom returns almost fifteen minutes later, he quickly apologises, before grabbing his jacket and ushering me out of the door to head to our table reservation. Hopefully, he has forgotten the conversation we had just been having and I can be saved from any more humiliation. As he holds the door open for me and I step out onto the decking, he puts a hand on my shoulder and I spin to face him. He pushes my hair to one side and whispers something into my ear.

Even over the loudness of the crashing waves and the wind gushing around us, his message is clear and rings in my ears like a sweet melody fifteen years too late.

"Don't ever think I didn't notice you."

*

After a night full of conversation and laughs, Tom walks me back to the cabin. I'd spent the most part of the night pretending to learn things about him that I already know. Although some things have changed as he's grown older, a lot hasn't. Back when Mark was dating my sister, he would be over at our house often. Mark talked about Tom a lot and it was clear to see that the two of them were close. I remember sitting at the dining table when I was fourteen as Mark chatted away to my parents over dinner, taking mental notes of Tom's likes and dislikes; his favourite TV shows, his favourite band, the places he liked to hang out. I tried my best to like the same things he did in hope that maybe it would make him notice me. I bought the T-shirts of the bands he liked and even forced Ali and Jenna to visit the local skate park every weekend for a month, but it didn't make him notice me, and I soon lost interest. After tonight, I realise I have more in common with him now than I ever did then, some might call it sods law. It was nice to relax and think about something other than Ali, even if it was only for a few short and admittedly selfish hours.

Tom leans against the doorframe to the cabin and I fumble in my handbag to fish out my key. The nervousness in my stomach that had vanished once in the restaurant has now returned threefold. He looks so calm, so casual and relaxed standing there. Then I realise that it's more than likely he's so calm is because he does this sort of thing all of the time, moving from one woman to the next then preying on his next victim. Dating was part of life to him, if that is what tonight was, a date. I'm not even sure anymore. Tom is sleek; he says the right things and acts the correct way, wooing women is simply woven into his DNA.

I, on the other hand, am not accustomed to the dating game, and I'm sure if I was, the rules would have changed dramatically since the last proper relationship I was in. Alex was Lucy's primary school teacher back when she was seven. He was a nice guy, but I had built my defenses up high and no amount of hard work, and dare I say love, would have brought them down back then. The relationship lasted eighteen months before I pushed Alex away completely. After that, my love life consisted of a few drunken one-night stands or some encounters that lasted a few weeks or a couple of months at the most, usually always based purely on sex. As soon as anything more serious started to emerge, I'd end it. It's easier that way.

I manage to find the key in the dim light and open the door. I turn to face Tom as he closes the inches separating us. The heat from his body penetrates my skin, his aftershave floats enticingly on the sea breeze. He reaches down and touches the side of my cheek, bringing his face close to mine. I force myself to move away.

"Good night, Tom," I say. "It was good catching up with you tonight."

Tom nods, apparently taking the hint that he is not invited in, here is where the night will end. He pushes his weight off the door frame and leans back in to kiss me on the cheek. My knees weaken at his touch as his face lightly brushes mine once more. He pauses briefly, then he moves away.

"Goodnight, Emily." I watch silently, as he walks off into the darkness.

Chapter 25

I'm only back in the cabin ten minutes when there's a knock on the door. I hesitate before I open it, half expecting to see Tom. Frantically, I start to think up an excuse in my head for him not to come in. *Do I really have one?* He never did seem the type to take no for an answer. The same nervous feeling mixed with exhilaration that I had earlier this evening hits me. I smooth my hair and straighten my top, taking a deep breath. When I open the door, it's Mark standing on the step in front of me. *Wrong brother.*

"Mark, hi, what are you doing here?" I ask, folding my arms across my chest as an unwanted disappointment hits me. I don't tell him that he has just missed his brother leaving.

"I've got some news for you, Em. I thought you would want to hear it face-to-face."

"Really, what news?"

"We've found Ali."

My heart rate increases. I invite Mark in and he follows me, perching himself on the edge of the couch.

"Is she okay?" I rush over and sit next to him.

"She's fine."

Relief washes over me. I can't remember the last time I felt like this. Maybe it was the time I lost Lucy when she was seven years old on a busy Long Sands beach and she showed up unscathed with an ice cream in her hand twenty minutes later at the lifeguard hut. I snap my attention back to Mark. "Where was she?"

"She's been in Somerset."

"Somerset? What was she doing there?"

"On holiday. She's been staying with a mutual friend of yours apparently, Jenna Stevens?"

My mind is working overtime "It was Jenna Cunningham when I knew her, but yes, she moved up to Bristol a while ago, must have relocated to Somerset," I offer bemused.

Mark nods. "Apparently unbeknown to any of us, the two of them have recently been back in touch. We weren't aware of that until now. Ali told us she went there to visit Jenna, said she needed to get away for a couple of weeks."

I think back to Ali's diary. She'd said she wanted to try and make contact with me and Jenna again. I didn't think she would have acted on it as soon.

"When did you speak to her?" I ask.

"I didn't. She called the station earlier when she saw an appeal for herself in an online local Sandbroke newspaper. She was more than a little confused when she called and spoke to Chrissy."

"But, what about the e-mail she sent me saying she was in trouble…"

"We are still looking into that part. Seems her e-mail account was hacked a little while ago and she lost her phone a week or so before she left for Somerset. It was only a cheap pay-as-you-go model. She wasn't bothered about modern technology, and nothing of any importance was stored on it, so she just replaced it with a new one, which explains why there was no answer when we tried contacting her. She didn't realise her e-mails had been hacked until we told her about the one sent to you. She doesn't use the account anymore."

I'm thoroughly confused.

"So, it was never really Ali who sent me the e-mail?"

"Nope."

"What about the clothes you found deserted on the beach, the book with her name in it?" I continue.

"We asked Ali about that. Our fear was that someone had been in her house and still has access. Ali told us the items that were found, including the book, had been amongst a load she donated as part of a charity jumble sale for the hospital. They could have been purchased by anyone and left on the beach by anyone. Ali was never on the beach that day. She was in Somerset with Jenna by then."

"What about her travelling there, though, how wasn't it picked up by the police? Surely they checked CCTV at the train stations and the airports. "

"She didn't get the train or fly. Jenna picked her up on the way back from an overnight stay for a business conference nearby. She hasn't been back to Cranley for a number of years. The only place she could remember was the beach club so she picked Ali up outside of there."

"And nobody saw the two of them there, or Jenna's car?"

"Seems not, but the area would have been deserted. It was before eight a.m. The beach club doesn't open until ten; there was nobody around. She paid for everything while she was away in cash, as she usually does, which is why there was no activity to pick up on her cards or accounts either."

I stare at Mark feeling bewildered. "I can't believe that she's just been staying with Jenna all this time." I slump back on the sofa and stare at him open mouthed.

Mark nods. "Me neither. Ali was totally unaware any of this was happening. She hasn't had any link to Cranley or Sandbroke since she left for Jenna's. No real need to for her to."

I sit forward and cross my legs under me, my brain back to working overtime.

"Hold on, though, that still doesn't explain the e-mail telling me she was in trouble or why her belongings seem like they were purposely left on the beach, someone still made it look like a disappearance," I say. I don't mention the messages and poster that I received too.

"The belongings could have just been a coincidence." Mark doesn't even remotely look like he believes his own words.

"Hell of a coincidence," I retort.

"Ali was very well-known for a long time when she was acting, Em. She told Chrissy that occasionally some people still recognise her now. She had quite a big following a few years back. It was probably just some daft super fan playing games with us."

"Why would a fan of hers send an e-mail to me, though? What part was I in it all?"

"I don't think you were. You were probably just the first name they came to in her e-mail address book. They possibly wanted to make someone aware to get the ball rolling with an investigation."

"But Mrs. Robertson was the one who reported it first, when Ali didn't show up to walk her dog. Not me."

"They wouldn't have been aware that Mrs. Robertson had been in touch, so they reached out to you instead."

"But Mrs. Robertson said she didn't show up to walk the dog."

"Mrs. Robertson was never really a reliable source. Ali told Chrissy that she carefully explained to Mrs. Robertson that she was going out of town for a couple of weeks so she wouldn't be able to walk the dog, but the poor woman must have forgotten Ali telling her that."

"I still don't understand, why would a fan want to fake Ali going missing? To go to all of this trouble?"

"Maybe they wanted to give her some exposure, to get her back in the spotlight like she once was. I've never understood how these people's minds work."

"No, me neither."

"Ali said she had a few cases back when she was living in London; fans following her, personal belongings going missing. Her accounts have been hacked a couple of times in the past, too. I don't think it's really that big a deal for her to be honest."

I smile, feeling a little more convinced.

"Ali is safe and well that is the main thing," says Mark.

"Yeah, you're right, it is."

Mark stands and makes his way to the door.

"Anyway, I have to get going. I just wanted to tell you the good news."

Mark makes his way to the door before he spins back to me.

"Oh, before I forget, Chrissy gave me this to pass on to you." He reaches into his pocket and hands me a business card with a mobile number written on the front. "Ali's new number. She said to give her a call. It's a shame you aren't sticking around to see her, but she knows you have to get home."

I take the card from him and give him an agreeable smile. "I know, it is unfortunate. I would have liked to have seen her. But you're right, I do need to get back to Newcastle. I've been here longer than I should already." I tuck the number in my pocket. "I'll give her a call when she is back and settled."

Mark smiles and opens his arms to give me a hug.

"Look after yourself, Mark," I say.

"You too, Emily. Please say hi to Trish for me."

"Will do."

"Have a safe trip back home."

"I will, thanks Mark. Take care."

Once again, I've passed up on the opportunity to tell Mark about the communication I believed was from Ali and I really can't say why. In my head, I'm telling myself that it was all purely harmless, as Mark has just suggested, and that maybe this person only had Ali's best interests at heart—they wanted nothing more than to get Ali back into the spotlight and restore her fame to what it once was. The text message and note must have all been sent to me by this yet-to-be-identified mystery fan of hers. Her phone was more than likely taken by this person, her e-mails hacked, the bag left on the beach and the photo delivered was all them too. Even the note tucked into the back of the framed picture in Ali's bedroom must have all been part of their plan. I suppose it wouldn't be too hard to do; if they followed Ali they could have easily slipped the note behind the frame. It had clearly been professionally printed, and more than likely framed for her too, maybe even delivered to her house, along with all the others on her bedroom wall. It could have been out of Ali's possession for a number of days, if not longer. The note could have been there a while and she would have never even known it was there.

The person I saw at the holiday park was clearly never Ali either. I briefly wonder if I had just wanted it to be at the time, and conclude that my mind had been playing tricks on me. Lack of sleep can easily play havoc with the brain function.

This fan of hers must absolutely idolize her, but, by the sounds of things, she isn't short of the odd admirer, which I find easy to understand. Her beauty and talent must be like a strong magnetic pull for some people.

Right now, all I need to concentrate on is that Ali is unharmed. It's all that matters. I can now willingly go home and return to my normal and unglamorous life.

I wave Mark off as he drives away from the cabin. A feeling of relief bubbling inside me, like a ton weight has lifted from my shoulders. Ali is safe and even though these past few days have been nothing but torture, something tells me our friendship has been rekindled and gives me hope for the future ahead.

I glance around the deserted park as Mark's taillights fade into the darkness and I start to close the cabin door. A sudden shiver runs the length of my spine as a gust of wind rushes past and for just a brief moment, even though I am fully aware it is only in my mind, I am suddenly overcome by the intense feeling that I'm being watched.

Chapter 26

"Ok Lucy, I'll see you tomorrow." I hang up the phone on my daughter and smile out to the sea. This time tomorrow I will be home with her and back to normality. Maybe we could get a movie and order a take away, sit in front of the television stuffing our faces and catching up. Approaching my last couple of days of being thirty-four, I can't say I have a lot to show for my years, but Lucy is worth more to me than anything in the universe and I can't wait to get home to see her.

The sky clouds over, casting shadows that drift slowly across the bay. Tiny drops of warm rain hit my face signaling to me that it's almost time to leave. A figure jogging along the shoreline runs in my direction, and only when he gets in my direct line of vision do I realise it's Tom. He stops in front of me as I rise to brush the sand off my legs.

"Hi Tom," I say.

"Hi Em, how you doing?"

"Feeling much better now, thanks." The conversation seems somewhat strained when compared to last night. I wonder if it's because I didn't respond the way he would have liked when he tried to kiss me. He's probably not used to getting knocked back by women. A blow to his almighty ego.

"Mark told me about Ali, it's great news," he says, looking down the beach then back to me.

"Yeah, it is," I reply.

"So you have nothing to be here for now."

His words sting, as I'm sure they were meant to, though reluctantly, I shake my head in response.

He nods, understanding as a drop of rain splashes onto his nose, followed quickly by another, then another. The heavens suddenly open.

Family's dash around us picking up towels and clothes draped on the sand. Most head towards Logan's Tavern to take shelter as the downpour takes hold.

"Come on." Tom grabs my hand and we join the crowds in the dash. Once inside, he pulls me towards the back of the bar where there is a small doorway. The door leads to a staircase, which opens out into an apartment.

"I didn't realise you lived above the bar," I say, taking a look around the large masculine open plan living space looking out over the sea.

"Yeah, it makes sense. I'm never away from the place," he answers, and I still detect a coolness in his voice. "Wait here, I'll get you a towel."

I push my dripping hair from my face and glance down at my soaked-through cotton dress. Goose bumps are fully raised on my wet skin as I wait. Tom returns, silently handing me a towel, with another draped around his own shoulders, his chest bare. He lets his eyes drift over my body, moving slowly from head to toe. He sees I notice and doesn't try to hide it. Only now am I aware that the fabric of my dress is soaked so much it has stuck to my body like a second skin, my underwear clearly visible. I cross my hands across my breasts unsure of where to look.

Without any form of warning, Tom takes a step closer to me, and using one arm, he pulls me toward him. He hesitates at first, but then his lips are on mine, and this time I don't stop him.

He kisses like I always imagined he would, soft and tender. His mouth moves passionately across my neck, his fingers in my wet hair, then moving down across my arms. He slips the straps of my dress from my shoulders and lets it fall in a sodden heap to the floor. His hands are on my body as mine are his; his skin is still damp. He pulls at my underwear as we move to the bedroom still in each other's arms. I no longer feel self-conscious.

We make love like two excited teenagers, fumbling over each other like it's our first time, lost in the moment, lost in each other. I find myself wondering if this is how I would have felt back then.

Afterwards, we take a shower together. Tom stands behind me trailing soft kisses across my shoulders, his fingers moving across my body tracing each curve, a clear expert with the female form. As the hot water rushes over me and I turn to kiss him, I let myself believe that this is real and that I'm not just another of his conquests, another notch on the bedpost, or a tally on his marker board.

For just a brief flicker in time, I pretend that he wants to be part of my life as much as I have always wanted to be part of his.

*

"I have to get going," I say to Tom. "I'm leaving first thing in the morning, and I need to get my stuff packed." It's getting dark outside now; I've no idea how long I've been here.

Tom stays silent. He's standing at the open doors leading onto a small balcony at the side of the apartment, his frame silhouetted by the glow of the setting sun ahead.

"You really have to go?" he asks finally, turning to look at me.

"Yeah, I do." My tone holds no emotion. Inside I'm trembling.

Tom sighs, leading me to feel an immediate and uncontrolled feeling of dislike towards him. I can't hold back what I'm thinking any longer.

"Oh, come on, Tom. Don't act like you are going to miss me, we both know what this was." I reach to pull up the now almost dry crumpled dress from the floor, then move to slip on my sandals.

"What do you mean?" he asks, looking heartily insulted. *Bravo on the acting skills, Mr. Logan, bravo!*

I sneer. "Don't insult my intelligence, Tom. You have always known how much I like you. Don't pretend you didn't. I was an easy lay for you. Nothing more."

Tom mildly erupts. "You think that's all you were? That's all I wanted from you since I saw you again the other night? To get you into bed?" He reaches where I am and I force myself to look up at him straight in the eye.

"Well, wasn't it?"

He shakes his head angrily. "You really don't know me at all, Em, do you?"

"Oh, come on Tom I was never on your radar at school and let's be honest, I'm still not. You don't have to pretend that this had any sort of meaning for you."

Tom smirks and says sarcastically, "You really think you have it all figured out, don't you?"

"And don't I?"

"You are so far off the mark. It's unbelievable," he snaps angrily.

"Really Tom? Because I'm not so sure I am."

"I'm not him, Em."

I look at the floor and talk to the wooden boards, "You're not who?" I whisper.

"Whoever the idiot is who has made you put your barriers up so high. Not let anyone in. I would never hurt you." Tom lowers his voice. He takes a step forward and I take one back. "Okay, I admit it maybe I should have approached you when we were younger. It wasn't that you weren't on my radar back then, but I was just a stupid kid. I felt that I had to follow the crowd to fit in and do what they expected me to do."

"And what about now?" I force myself to look up at him again.

He stares back into my eyes and doesn't look away. "Now, I think I'm falling for you."

I laugh out loud. My self-destruct button has once again been activated. I've been in this position a few times before and this time I feel is no different. Even though Tom is all I ever wanted, and this is perhaps a once in a lifetime opportunity to see if things could actually work, the only thing I can think of doing is to turn and run. So I do.

Chapter 27

So, the fabulous Ali Martin is alive and well and everyone is thrilled. How lovely. What you don't know is that every one of you has played directly into my hands and I now have you exactly where I want you. I'm the master of the chess board and you have all been nothing but my pawns.

I watched you again today as you sat alone on the beach in your own little world. No doubt it's carefree and happy there. It must be nice. I watched as Tom took you by the hand and led you to his apartment. I stood hidden in the shadows on the deserted beach as the rain fell, and saw you naked in each other's arms before you disappeared into the bedroom together. I hope you enjoyed yourself, Emily, and good for you that you have moved on with your life. I wish that it had been as easy for me.

I must admit, I didn't have you pegged as a slut. You were always so loyal when you were younger and I can only imagine that sleeping with strangers is nothing out of the ordinary to you these days. You didn't exactly look like a novice up there. I left you for a while and went to your cabin and had a good look around. You had left your handbag on the sofa. Once again, you have made this all too easy, Emily. After a quick look around and a few irresistible mind games, I found your purse and inside was exactly what I was looking for.

I waited as day turned to night. I watched as you left his apartment and ran back along the beach. You seemed in a hurry to get back up to the cabin, but this time, I didn't follow you. Tonight, I had more important matters to deal with.

Did you know that Tom Logan doesn't lock his doors at night? I know, I found it amusing that in this day and age, he feels secure enough not to have to bother. Which was good for me, because nobody in the busy bar noticed me slide away from my table and through the door to his apartment. He was standing with his back to me when I entered, still on the balcony where I wanted him to be. A fine figure of a man I must say, still in a state of half undress from the afternoon antics spent with you.

You don't know him at all Emily, not really.

He didn't even hear me approach, he was too busy watching you as you left. He looked like a love sick puppy dog. What a fool! By the time he realised that someone was there it was too late.

One shove is all it took. He went over the low balcony much quicker than I thought he would. The element of surprise certainly worked to my advantage. The fall wasn't that big and I knew it wouldn't be enough to kill him. Unfortunately. But it was sufficient enough to injure him, and judging by the way he fell, I know that I achieved that.

I have to admit, it gave me extreme satisfaction to know that I had hurt someone you love, because you do love him, don't you, Emily? You always have, ever since you were a kid, but we both know there's someone in this world that you love more, and now, I know her name. The picture you keep inside your purse of her is truly beautiful. You must be very proud. I know where she is now too.

You've made this all too easy, Emily. Not long now, Lucy. See you soon.

Chapter 28

There's a strange smell hanging in the atmosphere when I enter the cabin. It's a scent I recognise but can't place, musky and strong. As always, the air inside feels warm and sticky, causing beads of perspiration to immediately gather across my hairline and up my back the moment I step through the door.

I don't have much time to spare, so I rush straight to the bedroom and rip the empty rucksack from under the bed. There's a train leaving in half an hour that will get me home. It takes a longer route, but there's no point waiting until tomorrow. Especially not now. Ali is safe and on her way home, Tom's words yesterday were correct, there really is no real reason for me to be here anymore. Thoughts of Tom run through my head. I can still feel his lips on the arch of my neck, his touch on my skin and the pressure of his body against mine. Feeling aggravated, I quickly dismiss the memories and focus on the task at hand: To get back home and forget this whole mess even happened.

I thumb through my handbag to check I have the return tickets that I will need at the train station. I start to panic when I don't put my hand straight on them, then I find them tucked into a side pocket in the bag that I rarely use. *Strange, I can't remember putting them in there.*

I rush from room to room, throwing items in the bag and silently curse at myself for not being more organised. As I run to the kitchen, I notice shards of glass glistening on the floor and turn the corner to see my vase of flowers shattered in the centre of floor. Water seeps into the cracks of the floorboards, the flowers now wilting in the heat of the room. *I must have placed them too close to the edge of the sill. Maybe they fell off when the door slammed as I left earlier.*

In the kitchen, I rush round and do a quick clean up. I want to leave the cabin as tidy as possible; Claudia is a sweet girl I don't want to give her any more work than she already has. I complete a quick wipe down of the surfaces, rinse through the few dishes that I had left in the sink earlier, and discard of the broken glass from the vase. As I pass the fridge, I notice the poster of Ali is pinned to the door. Strange, I hadn't put it there. I know I'd left it on the kitchen bench when I returned from Logan's the other night.

Once again thoughts of Tom enter my mind; his hand trailing the back of my calf as he dressed my leg and my hand in his as we ran in the rain. I snap my attention back to the photo. *Claudia must have put it there when she was in cleaning this morning.* I take it from the fridge and pop in into my handbag. I'm sure Ali won't mind if I take this copy; it's a lovely photo of her. Even if it was possibly given to me by some psycho fan, it's too nice a picture to throw away.

Back in the bedroom, I empty the wardrobe and pick up a small pile of clothes from the floor, preparing to fold them. There's a hoodie amongst them that's not mine. I wonder where it came from at first, then I vaguely remember it being put around my shoulders the other day. I'm unsure if it belongs to Tom or Mark—both of them had lent me a jacket, neither of which I can remember handing back due to the distraught state I had been in on both occasions. I straighten it and lay it on the bed. I decide I'll leave it with Rose at reception when I check out.

As I finish packing my bag and begin folding the jacket something falls from the pocket. It's so small I almost don't see it. As I bend to pick up the small silver trinket a feeling of unease hits me. The hairs on the back of my neck rise to attention and an icy chill runs down my sweltering spine. A sickening realisation makes me wonder how I hadn't figured it out and questions how I could have been so utterly stupid. Suddenly, it all makes sense.

The train home will once again have to wait. Right now, there's somewhere I need to go.

Chapter 29

The police station is deserted—no big surprise this late in the evening. Nobody is manning the reception so I make my way straight through to the offices. I pass a couple of members of staff who ask me if they can help, but I wave them off rudely, and make my way to Mark's office. However, Mark is nowhere to be seen. Through the window I see Chrissy; she's sitting behind Mark's desk typing into a laptop. She's wearing a pair of black-rimmed glasses that reflect back the screen casting a blue glow across her face, and she has an immense look of concentration on her face

I burst into the office without knocking.

"I need to speak to Mark," I say to Chrissy breathlessly. Fury rages inside me, and the walk here has only added fuel to an already raging fire in my mind.

She stands from behind the desk as soon as she notices me and moves in my direction. "He's just gone home for the night," she says, wheeling a chair over to me, silently offering me a seat. I sit down heavily, my knees are shaking. I cross one leg over the other and try to stop the nervous tapping of my foot.

"Will you call him for me? I need to speak to him."

"Are you okay, Em?" asks Chrissy. She removes her glasses and places them on top of her head.

I get to my feet, unable to sit still. "Did you know?" I snap.

"I'm sorry, Emily, did I know what?" Her face says it all. She knew.

"Stop fucking around, Chrissy. Did you know about Ali and Mark?"

Chrissy's cheeks turn slightly pink. She calmly closes the screen of the laptop and sighs as she plants her feet and meets my disgusted stare.

"Yes, I knew," she admits immediately, keeping her voice low.

I shake my head angrily. The office is starting to swim around me, and I sit back down and grip the sides of the chair feeling nauseous. Another officer pops his head around the open door, fixing his attention on Chrissy.

"Everything alright, Chris?" he asks, blatantly nodding at me as if I am some sort of problem source.

"Yeah, fine, Tony, I'll see you tomorrow," she answers confidently. He smiles and leaves after giving me a final unsure glance. Chrissy closes the door after him and makes sure that there is nobody around.

"It's probably not what you think Emily," she says quietly.

"Oh, really, Chrissy? And what's that? That your partner, the man in charge of the investigation into Ali's disappearance, was having an affair with her?" I stand up again and meet Chrissy's eye. "Why didn't he tell me?"

"Because it was over a while before she seemingly disappeared. There was no point in him being part of it, he had no involvement in her apparent disappearance Emily."

"How can you be so sure?" I feel betrayed that Mark didn't feel he could tell me about him and Ali.

"Oh, come on, Emily, it was all a huge misunderstanding. You know that now. The bloke wouldn't hurt a fly. You know that as much as I do."

"What about his wife? Does she know about their affair?" Feeling sickened, I pick up the picture of Mark's family from the desk and thrust it in her face.

Chrissy takes the photo and carefully places it back down on the desk. "Mark's wife Kim died almost two years ago. Breast cancer."

I am speechless for a few moments and stand gawping at Chrissy before finally finding my words again. "He... he didn't say."

"Yeah, still struggling with losing her. Ali was the first woman he has gotten close to since losing Kim. They had a brief relationship, but Mark felt too guilty to carry it on, even after well over a year. He still found it hard to move on from losing his wife. Felt like he was betraying her memory in some way."

"But he still wears a wedding band."

"Hasn't quite got round to taking it off yet. Anyway, it only lasted a few months. He finished things with Ali a couple of months back."

"It might have been brief, but Ali really cared for him. She thought it was serious."

"That may have been the case, and I believe he really cared for her too, but the timing was all wrong."

"How has he managed to be in charge of the investigation and not let on? Surely it was hard for him?"

"He's been beating himself up since he found out Ali was missing. He made damn sure both of us were actively involved with the investigation. Much more so than we normally would in other missing person's cases like Ali's. We've been working day and night to find her. He swore he wouldn't stop until he did. It's been killing him inside."

"Who else knows he was seeing her?" I ask. I pray that she doesn't say Tom's name. I can't cope with him keeping this from me too.

"Just me," says Chrissy. I let out a breath that I didn't even realise I was holding.

"Mark broke down one day and told me everything. He's a good guy, Emily, he wanted to find her as much as you and I did. In all honesty, I think it's made him see how much he cares for Ali. I think he's starting to regret ever finishing things with her."

I nod.

"How did you find out about them, Emily?" Chrissy asks, narrowing her eyes at me suspiciously.

I don't answer.

"You may as well come clean. I spoke to Ali earlier. I know she hasn't spoken to you yet so she couldn't have told you about her and Mark."

Shit! I close my eyes and leave them closed before I reopen them. "I went to her house." I whisper. Chrissy looks shocked.

"Damn it, Emily. Why didn't you tell us you had been there?"

"I found a diary she kept and read it," I continue. "Ali mentioned a man she was involved with, but there was never a name, then I found out it was Mark. Just a little while ago."

"How did you find out it was him?"

"A charm she mentioned he had given her fell out of the pocket of a jacket he lent me the other day, after I'd been in hospital."

Chrissy purses her lips. Placing her hands on her hips, she looks at the floor and begins to pace as if trying to figure out her next move.

"That's not all," I continue. I know that I'm in deep shit as it is so I may as well continue and tell Chrissy the rest. "I've had a couple of notes, a text message was sent to my phone, and a poster delivered to me at the cabin that I didn't tell you about. I even though I saw her at one point, but I was obviously wrong about that."

Chrissy's head snaps back up. "God, Emily, why the hell didn't you tell us? You know that withholding information from the police is a criminal offence, don't you?" She's understandably angry.

I take a gulp. My throat is dry and scratchy. *That's rich coming from her tonight!* She and Mark have withheld their fair share of information too, and they *are* the police.

"I thought it was her. That Ali was sending me things and she said not to tell anyone. I worried that she was in trouble. She asked me not to go to the police. So I didn't."

Chrissy nods and seems to mellow, slightly.

"Mark thinks it's just some fan of hers who tried to get an investigation started to get Ali back in the limelight," I say.

Chrissy continues to pace the small amount of floor space in the office and stays silent a few moments while she thinks. "Yeah, we've discussed that could be a possibility," she answers. "But that was without the addition of the other messages sent to you. To me, it now seems that you may be more of a target than Ali was. Is there anybody who could have been messing with you Emily, anybody who would want you torment you as they have been doing the past few days?"

"No," I say, immediately.

"Anybody who would want to get you back to Sandbroke maybe?"

I go to answer, then suddenly, the smell in the cabin tonight barges its way to the front of my mind. The feeling that someone was watching me, the train tickets in the wrong place, the photo on the fridge, the flowers from another man spread in a shattered vase across the kitchen floor. I feel myself start to tremble. Chrissy grabs my elbow and sits me back down as my balance is lost.

"How could I have been so stupid?" I ask. Chrissy already has her phone out of her pocket and on the desk, a pen is poised in her hand in preparation for what I am about to tell her. "He did all this to get me back here. He wanted to see me so he's been following me and watching me."

"Who is it, Emily? Who's behind all this?"

There's no doubt in my mind now. The person I thought I had left in my past has caught up with me. The smell in the cabin earlier is the same aftershave he used to wear back when we were together, the heavy musky fragrance I've tried so hard to vanquish from my mind. He's come back. He's found me. Just like part of me always knew he would. The messages, the text, the notes; it's all been him. I take a deep breath and tears fill my eyes.

"I think it's one of my ex-boyfriends," I say. "His name's Jake. Jake Saunders."

Chapter 30

I'm now on the train back to Newcastle. After telling Chrissy everything yesterday, I knew the logical thing to do was to get out of Sandbroke and get back to my family as quickly as possible. If all of this has been Jake playing games, as Chrissy thinks it could have been, then the safest place for me is back home and away from Sandbroke. I've lived in the North East for over fifteen years and he's never traced me, so nothing makes me believe he would be able to now. I'm getting away from him. For good this time. Jake had always been a huge game player when we were together. He enjoyed having control over those around him. Pulling a stunt like this was right up his street and I am annoyed at myself for playing straight into his hands.

I had tried desperately to get home last night, but Chrissy had to follow procedure and take statements from me. Even though she rushed through as fast as she could, I was still far too late to catch the last train. I had checked the nearest airport to see if I could get a last-minute flight, but there was no availability at such short notice.

I'm four hours into the train journey home when Mark calls me to tell me Tom has been in an accident, that it looks as though he fell from his balcony, and even though neither of us say anything we both know what each other are thinking. Jake. He had fallen from the side balcony of his apartment and was found by one of the tavern's waitresses, unconscious. He is in hospital now. He's awake with three broken ribs and a fractured wrist, but can't remember a thing about what happened. Mark assures me that he's fine and it could have been a lot worse. I feel sick.

"I'm sorry I didn't tell you about me and Ali," says Mark, before we end the call.

"Me too," I reply. "But I kind of see why you didn't."

"Thanks, Em." Mark's breath shudders and I imagine him closing his eyes. I'd never really stopped to think about how hard this must have been on him. Mark just isn't the sort to date a woman and not form any kind of feelings for her. I refuse to believe that he was as cold-hearted as Ali made out in her diary.

"I'm sorry for not being honest about the messages and about Ali's diary. If I had been, you might have put two and two together and realised that it was never really Ali sending them to me at all."

"Do you still have the diary?" Mark asks directly.

"It's on a memory stick. I left it with Chrissy at the station last night. Please apologise to Ali when you give it back to her. I feel like I've invaded her privacy reading it."

"I'm sure she won't mind, given the circumstances."

"She really cares for you Mark," I blurt out. I can't help myself, the words are out of my mouth before I have time to process them properly. I know that really it's none of my business.

Mark ignores my statement and quickly changes the subject as he proceeds to tell me they are looking into the possibility that it was Jake sending the messages to me.

"We're looking for Jake now," Mark says. Seems he left Sandbroke a few months after you did, and he was bragging around the town that he was moving away to be with the woman he loved. We all assumed back then that was you. That's where the confusion came from, why everyone in Sandbroke thought you had moved away together."

"Nope, he definitely didn't go anywhere with me. I left Sandbroke to get away from him," I confess.

"Yeah, I'd guessed that. Why didn't you tell me?"

"I don't know. The embarrassment I suppose. I was an idiot for staying with him as long as I did. Nobody liked him. I was the only one who didn't see him for what he really was."

"You have nothing to be embarrassed for," says Mark. "So who did he leave town with?"

"He had a few women on the go while he was in a relationship with me. You could take your pick from them.".

"I'm sorry you had to go through that, Em, he sounds like a horrible piece of work. I hate to bring all this back up, but do you know anyone he may still be in contact with?"

"Not a clue, I stopped caring a long time ago."

"I understand. Well, we'll keep digging. If it was him, then he couldn't be far."

"Keep me posted, Mark. I want to know what's going through that bastard's mind as much as you do."

"Will do, Em, look after yourself."

I hesitate before I speak again. "Mark?"

"Yeah."

"Will you tell Tom I hope he's better soon?" I pause and take a deep breath before I continue, "and that I'm sorry."

"Sorry about what?"

"Sorry about everything." I flush, even though he can't viably see me. I know that Mark and Tom are close and Tom is likely to have already told him about what happened between us last night.

Mark doesn't deny he knows about it and keeps his reply as noticeably casual as possible, most probably to avoid any more disgrace on my part. "Gotcha, no probs. I will."

"Thanks, Mark."

"Bye for now, Em."

"Bye."

Tears prick my eyes as I hang up on Mark. A little while later, the familiar overcast skies, the famous bridges and tall city buildings creep into view as the train makes its way over the River Tyne on its approach to the station. It's late afternoon now, and I imagine the city centre bustling full of Saturday afternoon shoppers; a comfort of knowing I'm home floods in around me. I'm on the station platform, making my way to the exit, when my phone text alert sounds, probably Lucy. She was going shopping today and said she would meet me at the station, she'll be waiting outside. I can't wait to see her. These past few days have only made me appreciate how lucky I am to have what I do. So what if I have a job that doesn't pay well or a home that isn't a gleaming mansion like Ali's? It's my home and that's all that matters. I won't ever question it again.

I reach into my handbag, but when I pull out my phone and study the display, I see it's not a message from Lucy, but looking at the unknown number, I know instantly that it's from the same phone that I received the text from earlier in the week. My hand shakes as I press the button to open the photo attached to a blank text message.

Time slows around me and the busy station begins to move in slow motion as a photo of my daughter shopping in the city centre taken an hour ago, emerges onto the screen.

Chapter 31

"For Christ's sake Mark, pick up your damn phone!" I shout loudly into my mobile. People passing by on the train station platform stare at me. I'm hysterical now and am well beyond the point of caring. A station guard spots me and begins to approach me cautiously.

"Are you alright, pet?" I ignore the man and turn my back to him, moving further along the platform. Announcements blare over the station speakers alerting travellers to a delay on the 15:59 service to London Kings Cross. People continue to rush around me; the strong smell of black coffee and greasy pasties from a nearby café hits me and forces me to stop as I gag. *He has my daughter. I know he has her.*

I imagine Jake and Lucy meeting. Jake will coax her into a false sense of security, something he was always been good at. That's why nobody in Sandbroke knew what he was really like, not completely. He would put on an act and easily fool them all into believing he was the best thing on this earth. He also had a wildly possessive personality, and I know that if he gets his hands on her he will know straight away she is his daughter and once that happens there isn't a chance in hell he would let her go.

Finally, Mark picks up.

"Hi Em, I was just about to call you," he says, oblivious to the bordering psychotic state I have entered.

"He has my daughter, Mark," I blurt out. My voice is raised, attempting to overpower the sound of the station announcements and the louder sound of my own heart pounding in my ears.

"Your daughter?" Mark asks, clearly taken aback. "I didn't know you had a daughter."

"Yes, Lucy. She's fifteen."

Mark pauses. "Okay, calm down, Em. Who has your daughter?"

"Who do you think? Jake. He's here, he knows she would be here. He found out somehow. She's his daughter, Mark, but I never told him. He's going to take her. I know it." My words are coming out rushed and muddled. I'm trying to make sense and I'm praying that Mark can grasp what I'm trying to tell him. He responds quickly.

"Emily, Emily please slow down."

"He must have got the last train here last night, or a flight to make it here before me. He found out where I live, Mark, and tracked down Lucy." I look around the station frantically.

"Emily, stop, Jake doesn't have your daughter and he isn't in Newcastle," says Mark.

"What do you mean? He sent me a photo of her, he—"

"That's what I was about to call to tell you. Jake is in prison, Em. Has been for a while and will stay there for a very long time..."

"What? Prison? But..." My head spins.

"He's been in and out for years. Drugs, GBH, ABH you name it, he's been charged with it. Then, a year ago, he was involved in a car accident. He was driving under the influence and wrapped his car around a tree. He got away unharmed, but his passenger died at the scene." Mark pauses and I hear him taking a sharp intake of breath before he continues. "The passenger was his daughter, twelve years old. He refused to admit responsibility. He killed his own child."

"God, that's horrible." I put my free hand to my mouth and desperately try to pull my mind away from his poor daughter for the time being simply because I know I have to focus on my own.

"Hold on, so he hasn't been in Sandbroke either?" I ask, now thoroughly confused.

"Nope. Impossible."

"So then who has been sending me the notes, the photo? If it wasn't Jake, then who?" My mind races. Anger rips through me.

"That's what we are trying to find out, Em."

"Someone has taken a photo of my daughter, Mark, it was only today. They sent it through to my phone a couple of minutes ago. Lucy isn't answering her phone and she always answers her phone. Something's happened. I need to get to her." I can hear the desperation in my own voice.

"Where are you now? Are you still on the train?" asks Mark. I can hear him moving around the police station as the background voices emerge.

"No. I've just arrived. I'm at Newcastle Central Station."

"Okay, stay there. I'll get on to Northumbria police and explain what happened. They'll come and get you and take you to find your daughter. It's not safe for you to go alone."

I'm crying now, sobbing as people continue to stare. "Okay."

"Don't worry, Em, it's just someone playing games with you. We'll catch the psycho, you can take my word for it."

I take a deep breath and try to steady my shaking voice. "I hope so, Mark. I really hope so."

Part Six

Chapter 32
Lucy

I press my face close to the glass display cabinet and pick out the prettiest thing I can see that falls within my small price range—a silver necklace with a small mother of pearl heart attached. I ask the shop assistant behind the counter to wrap it as nicely as she can. I tap my fingers against the glass as the girl fiddles with pink bows and sparkly love heart confetti. I'm conscious of the time. Mum's train will be arriving soon and I said I would be at the station to meet her. My phone battery has died, no doubt she is trying to call. She'll kill me when she sees me. I'm sure she'll cheer up when she opens her present.

I'm buying the gift partly because it's her birthday in a couple of days' time and partly because I want to apologise. I haven't been totally truthful with her these past couple of months. When she arrives home from visiting Auntie Trish in Scotland, I intend to tell her that I have spent the last couple of months searching for my dad behind her back. I've spent hours on the Internet researching him. It took a little while, but then I found out his name. Once I had that, it didn't take long to learn more about him.

Up until recently, I've had no reason to want to find out who my father is but I suppose curiosity finally got the better of me. I now know my dad's name is Jake Saunders, that he's thirty-eight years old, and originally from Manchester. He lived in Sandbroke where my mum grew up for a couple of years before moving and settling in Yorkshire. I have his big blue eyes and the exact same skin tone.

At first, I was excited and even thought about arranging to meet him. But then I did a bit more digging was disgusted with what I found out. I now know he isn't a nice man in fact, he's not far off being a monster; he has done some very bad things and he is currently in prison in Leeds. He was charged a year ago with killing his daughter. Mia was only a few years younger than me. I've often wondered what it would be like to have a brother or sister, not that I'm grumbling. I've been brought up as an only child and I can't complain about the family that I have. I know now that Mum didn't tell me about my dad to protect me. She probably is unaware that I had a half-sister and I understand that. I wish I hadn't started looking and that I never found out who my dad was.

I know that you have been following me for the past ten minutes. Don't bother trying to hide because I know now who you are; I saw your picture in the same newspaper archive that told me my dad was a murderer.

I step out of the jewellers and purposefully bend to tie my shoelace to check you are still there. At first I think that you have gone, but then I catch a glimpse of you through the crowds. You've changed your hair colour from what it was in the newspaper photo, but I have a good memory for faces and I can tell instantly it's definitely you. I continue walking, quickening my pace in the direction of the train station. As soon as I get there I'll tell Mum everything and explain that I think you are here, she'll know what to do. I try my best to get through the crowds of shoppers winding my way through the bodies in an attempt to shake you off. But I know it's too late, I've been stupid and run out of time. You have reached me.

I know you are there before I even turn around. There's a shift in the air, the wind changes its direction ever so slightly, but just enough to make me aware you're behind me. I don't dare turn to look at you. I want to pretend that I'm imagining it, but the busy street is full of people and I don't want to make any more commotion for them than is necessary.

I calmly place my bags of shopping on the pavement trying my best to avoid the stares from passersby who have noticed that something isn't quite right. I look down at the beautifully wrapped parcel that sits on the ground, its paper packaging now soaking up the rain from the damp pavement. In it is a necklace, a birthday present. I was looking forward to seeing her face when she opens it. That's not going to happen now.

A little girl of about seven years old clutching a large brown fuzzy teddy bear comes out of the store next to me. Her tightly curled hair is pulled into pigtails secured with bright pink grips. She smiles sweetly, then looks puzzled as her mother mutters something, then drags her quickly away.

I still have my back to you, but I can now see a reflection in the shop window that I am standing near. The image is blurred in its rain streaked glass. I watch silently as you take a step closer to me and raise an item from inside your jacket pocket, the hazy sun shines against it and I realise it's a small handgun. Although I'm shocked, I knew there was a possibility that this day was going to come.

Now panic sets in around us.

"It's a gun," I hear a man shout from somewhere close.

"Someone call the police," another yells loudly.

People start to run. The sound of screaming rings loudly in my ears. The busy street quickly clears, now becoming too quiet and extremely eerie for a Saturday afternoon in a normally busy city centre.

"How did you find me?" I ask, still with my back to you. My voice shakes, as does my whole body.

You don't answer.

I close my eyes. Tears start to stream down my cheeks, fear raging inside of me, or is it fury? I can hear sirens in the distance. Their noise gets gradually louder. Help is on its way, but it's too late now, you have hold of me around the neck. I don't attempt to try and get free. I'm too traumatised. Too frightened. My knees give way, but your hold prevents me from falling to the ground.

Your grip is so tight I can't breathe. With one hand you grab hold of my hair, wrenching my head painfully to one side. *1,2,3 wake up, 1,2,3 wake up!*

But this isn't another dream. The silent and desperate plea to my subconscious won't work this time.

I scream out as you put the gun to my temple. The cold hard metal penetrates through my skull. Your breath is heavy and hot on my ear. Your breathing is fast, but still you don't speak.

I close my eyes squeezing them shut as tightly as I can, waiting for the trigger to be drawn. The bullet. My death. But it doesn't come as quickly as I thought it would.

Police sirens grow louder and blue lights now blaze behind my eyes as I wait for the sound that is going to be the last thing I ever hear. There is no bright light for me to enter. There are no angels or lost loved ones waiting—maybe they will come later. I don't see all the significant times of my life; specific memories, important life milestones or the people in my life that I hold dearest. Instead, my mind is clear and calm. I'm not afraid anymore. I'm ready.

Then suddenly, I hear it, the deafening bang. A noise that vaguely sounds like my own voice crying out echoes in my ears as I fall towards the damp pavement. The police sirens sound fades away. The light behind my eyes weakens as I continue to fall. Then I see nothing but darkness.

I don't feel myself hit the ground.

Chapter 33

The police are waiting for me by the time I get to the station exit. Mark has done his job well; they are fully briefed on my case and eager to find my daughter as soon as possible. They quickly usher me into the back of a parked patrol car.

"Hi, Emily, I'm Police Constable Reynolds, Northumbria Police," a youngish looking girl, with pinned-back mid-length blonde hair says to me. She turns in the front of the car so she can make eye contact from the front seat as the car pulls away. "And this is Sergeant Callaghan." She points to the older officer driving the car next to her who has a shaven head and an overly stern look on his face. His uniform is stretched tightly over a huge set of shoulders and broad torso. I can't help thinking that on first appearance, he looks like he should be on the opposite side of the law to the one he chooses to enforce as a profession.

"Inspector Logan has been in touch and told us what has happened. Can I take a look at the photo you told him you received?" asks Reynolds.

I nod and pull my mobile from my pocket to hand to her. She inspects it then passes the phone to Callaghan, who takes a quick look at the photo of Lucy and hands me back the phone over his left shoulder before setting his eyes back to the road ahead.

"The photo was taken just over an hour ago Serg," says Reynolds to Callaghan, who nods in response.

"Looks like it was taken just off Northumberland Street," adds Callaghan. "What makes you think something has happened to your daughter, Miss Moore?" His voice is softer than I imagined it would be, given his size. Though it comes nowhere close to settling me.

"I've been trying to call her but she's not answering, I just know something isn't right. They sent me the photo to warn me they are watching her."

"Is there anybody you know who would have any reason to want to harm your daughter?"

"No, I thought it could be her father, but I was wrong."

"Well, you've done the right thing. Hopefully whoever this is has not approached her." Officer Reynolds gives me a reassuring smile which doesn't work. I rub at my eyes that are sore and swollen and tug at the collar of my shirt that seems to be threatening to strangle me. My head is banging, tension cuts through my shoulders and up my neck like a tightening vise. Officer Reynolds begins to ask me questions about Lucy as we near the street where her photo was taken; height, weight, and clothes she is wearing. Her voice seems distant and slow like she's trying to talk under water. Although they have now seen the photo, to them it's not very obvious. The photo isn't in very good focus and the quality of it doesn't look like it was produced on an expensive, flashy camera phone like everyone is used to seeing these days. Mark did say that Ali's old phone was just a cheap model, so it makes sense that this could be from the phone that was more than likely stolen from her. To me, the photograph is as clear as crystal.

I'm aware that I need to call my mum and dad, at the same time I don't want to worry them unnecessarily and I am conscious it will take up valuable minutes.

"Five-two, petite, slim build, long blonde hair, blue eyes, wearing blue stone-wash skinny jeans, a plain white vest top, looks like she has her pink hoodie tied around her waist and she's wearing her white Converse trainers." I'd worked overtime at the restaurant for a month to save up to get those trainers for her. You would have thought I had given her a thousand pounds, she was so grateful when I presented them to her last month. I wipe at my watery eyes and finish rattling off Lucy's description as Sergeant Callaghan bends and speaks into a radio.

We continue through the city centre. I carefully study every young girl I see who looks even a little like Lucy as we pass, hope builds and then quickly drops, breaking just like the ocean waves at Ceaders Bay on a rough day.

"Do you know where Lucy was heading?" asks Reynolds.

"She said she was doing some shopping." I move the seatbelt away from my neck, finding it increasingly more difficult to breathe.

"Do you know which shops she was going to?"

"No idea. Her grandpa was dropping her in the centre at noon." I think of my dad and how hard it has been cutting the apron strings when it comes to Lucy. The fact he had even let her go looking around the shops alone for a couple of hours is a pure miracle.

"She didn't mention what she was shopping for?" asks Reynolds.

"No. It's my birthday in a few days, so it was probably a present for me." Guilt rips through me painfully. "She was coming to the station to meet me off the train, but she would have been there by the time the train got in; she's never late."

"Okay, well, we have an officer at the station, just in case," Callaghan says.

"Thank you." I turn back to the window to continue looking for Lucy.

There is a loud crackling on the radio attached to Reynolds. It continues loudly for a few seconds, then stops before it sparks back to life and I hear a voice. I can't quite make out what the person on the other side of the radio is saying. It's a mixture of police terms and a language that I am sure is English, but my sheer state of despair won't allow me to decipher. Officer Reynolds turns to face me, a concerned look now on her face. I instantly start to panic.

"What's wrong, what's happening?" I ask. Callaghan steps on the accelerator and the car shoots forward as he presses something and a siren starts to sound. That's the moment I learn that there's been reports of a suspect with a gun, pointing it at a young girl on a road based near the city's main shopping district matching Lucy's description.

Chapter 34

The siren blares. Blue flashing lights reflect brightly against the rain drenched ground. By the time we get there, I can barely breathe and am furiously fighting against passing out. I hear the gunshot as we round the corner to get to the street where Lucy has been sighted, and scream out loudly. It seems to take an eternity for us to get to her. Once there, Sergeant Callaghan brings the car to an abrupt halt in the middle of the road. He gets out of the car and runs to the scene now directly ahead of us. Officer Reynolds holds back and turns to check on me.

"I need air," I hear myself say. She hesitates briefly before she gets out of the car and opens my door. I throw up violently on the roadside as soon as the fresh air hits me. *God, let my daughter be ok.*

In the distance, a little farther down the street, Sergeant Callaghan reaches a group of police officers already at the scene where he tries to help to control a growing crowd of people who have started to gather around the area. There are numerous police cars dotting the road and an ambulance is parked farther back on the pavement. I struggle at first to see what the crowd of people is focusing on, then I see a body covered over by a green sheet in the centre of the path. *No, please, no.*

Without thinking, I start to run. I can hear Officer Reynolds shouting at me, but that just makes me quicken my pace. I use all the force I have to burst through the crowds of people until I reach a group of officers at the front who stop me dead in my tracks. Sergeant Callaghan appears next to them and takes me lightly by the arm, moving me to one side. "We are trying to find out exactly what has happened," he says calmly. More police arrive and soon the area is starting to clear as people are quickly evacuated from the street as roads are closed and the area is cordoned off.

"I need to see my daughter," I shout at Callaghan. I can't take my eyes off her body on the ground, small and fragile. I see now that there is blood mixing into the surrounding puddles turning them a deep shade of crimson. I imagine Lucy underneath, her beautiful long golden hair now patched in red soaking up the muddy water from the puddles that have formed. I bend over and clutch my stomach.

Officer Reynolds appears from nowhere by my side and Sergeant Callaghan leaves me again, heading towards the ambulance.

"Who did this?" I scream at Reynolds. "Who killed my daughter?" I look at her, pure despair pulsating through my veins, willing to accept nothing more than a truthful direct answer. When she doesn't answer immediately, I feel myself getting hysterical again.

"What are you still doing here? Why aren't you trying to catch the person that did this?" I shove Reynolds hard in the chest, forcing her to stumble backwards. She steadies herself and moves quickly back to my side before draping her arm over my shoulders. I'm aware of a horrible, high pitched voice wailing my daughter's name over and over, and it takes a little while to realise the awful noise is coming from me. Then I hear another sound, at first I think I'm imagining it. Most likely my mind playing tricks on me, allowing the impossible to happen; for time to turn back on itself.

"Mum." I whiz around, confused, trying to detect where the noise is coming from, setting my sights once again at the body on the ground. "Mum." There it is again, louder this time. Then I see Sergeant Callaghan again, making his way over from the ambulance. He has his arm around someone—Lucy. My legs lose their support and I fall helplessly to my knees on the damp pavement as Lucy shakes off Callaghan's grip. She reaches me within seconds and flings her arms around my neck. She's crying and clearly distraught, but other than that she doesn't seem to have a scratch on her.

"Your daughter's fine, Miss Moore," says Callaghan, reaching us. Lucy buries her head into my neck and continues to weep.

"Thank you, thank you," I shout to nobody and everybody at the same time.

"The suspect did grab Lucy." He lowers his voice and moves away slightly as if trying to prevent Lucy from hearing him. "But then they turned the gun on themselves. Your daughter fainted, but otherwise she is unharmed. She wasn't fully conscious when the shooting took place." He moves in front of us to purposefully block Lucy's view of the body on the ground. I'm crying loudly now, tears of joy and sheer relief that she is unharmed. That she is alive.

"I'm so sorry for leaving you," I whisper into Lucy's ear.

"It's alright, Mum, I'm fine, honestly," she answers, pulling back and wiping the tears from her face. *There she is, my strong little girl.* Officer Reynolds steps forward and rubs Lucy affectionately on the arm.

"Let's go and get you a cup of tea and a seat," she says to Lucy, taking her and guiding her away from the scene. "I'll make sure Inspector Logan is updated too," she adds.

"Thank you," I mouth, this time only to her as they disappear behind the ambulance. The area has now been completely evacuated, apart from police and myself.

"Who is under that sheet?" I ask Callaghan, finally managing to compose myself a little.

"We were hoping you could tell us," he answers.

I nod, understanding what he is asking of me.

"We don't have to, if you don't feel up to it," he adds.

"No, I'll do it."

Callaghan steps forward and pulls up the incident tape cordoning off the section of pavement where the body lies. He holds it for me to pass under, then kneels down at the body and slowly lifts the blanket. He only needs to move it a few centimeters before a gasp catches sharply in my chest and for me to know the identity of the person underneath.

211

Chapter 35
Mark

I hang up the phone after speaking to the police in Newcastle. Chrissy enters the office and hands me a cup of tea.

"Cheers Chris." I rub at my head. It's been banging since Ali disappeared, or at least, since we were led to believe she had disappeared. Whoever was behind this was doing a damn good job of keeping us all on our toes.

"You should go home and get some rest, Mark. You look like shit," she says as she takes a seat opposite me. "There's not much you can do here, we are waiting for Ali to return to Sandbroke before we can question her and I'm sure they have things under control up in Newcastle."

"Thanks for not mincing your words as usual, Chrissy," I reply.

She half-smiles, a look of genuine concern on her face. "Well, it's true, you look absolutely terrible."

I take a sip of tea and do my best not to let the mention of Ali's name set my heart racing. I've tried not to get personally involved with this case, to remain professional. I'm lucky I've still got my job and I know that the only reason I do is Chrissy.

If it hadn't been for her holding everything together recently, I have no doubt I would have broken down.

The truth is I've not only lied to the police about my involvement with Ali, but I've also lied to myself over how I really feel about her. The thought that something could have happened to her has taken its toll on me these past couple of weeks.

"You spoke to Emily again yet?" Chrissy asks, breaking my trail of thought.

"No, she's with the police now. They are looking for her daughter as we speak."

"Did you even know she had a daughter?"

"Not till twenty minutes ago when she told me."

Chrissy leans back in the seat and stares at the ceiling, the ultra-bright fluorescent lighting makes her skin look even paler than usual.

She brings her eyes back to me. "I hope they find her."

"Yeah, me too."

"Who would want to do this?"

"It seemed logical that it was Jake," I reply.

"I agree, Mark. Now we know all the facts. It seemed the most plausible option. He uses Ali to get Emily to come back to Sandbroke, because he knew that she would never come back without a good reason," Chrissy admits. "And Ali was the best reason, he could use. She clearly thinks a lot of her old friend."

I nod. "Emily gets back here, and he spends time playing games to keep her here a bit longer—"

"Then he unexpectedly finds out he has a daughter he knew nothing about and tracked her down," Chrissy interrupts.

"But Jake has been locked up for a while now."

"So then who…"

"Your guess is as good as mine, Chrissy. Do me a favour and have a closer look into the death of Jake's daughter. Maybe there's more to it."

Chrissy gets up and rubs her eyes, she looks as wrecked as I feel.

"On it." She smiles and squeezes my shoulders as she passes and leaves the office. A few minutes later there's a knock on my door.

"What's up Rach?" I ask, as one of the station receptionists pops her head around the door.

"Sorry to bother you, Mark, you have a visitor waiting in reception, she says she wants to speak to you." I don't need to ask who it is. I stretch in my seat and stand to follow Rachael through to the station entrance.

Ali stands alone in the corner with a nervous smile on her face. She's wearing a patterned summer dress that falls to her knees. Her dark hair has lightened since I saw her last and cascades over her bare shoulders. She looks as beautiful as ever. I feel an invisible pull to her that I haven't felt in the months since we last saw one another.

"Ali, hi, how are you?" Instinct makes me lean towards her as if to kiss her, I stop myself as soon as I realise what I'm doing.

"Hi, Mark, I'm good thanks." I can hear the nerves lacing her voice. She takes a step back, a small flush of pink emerging on her sun-kissed cheeks.

"I just wanted to see how everything is going. Your officers briefed me on what happened when I returned home from my trip this morning. I am so sorry about everything."

I bury my hands deep into my pockets and make more space between us. If I don't I fear I will reach out and take her in my arms. I shouldn't have let her go.

"Not your fault, you weren't to know," I say. My voice comes out harsher than I intended it to.

"How's Emily?" she asks.

"Justifiably, not great."

"Do you have any idea who it could have been, who set everything up to make it look like I'd disappeared?" Her voice trails off and she visibly shudders.

"We were hoping that you could help us on that one."

"I really have no idea, Mark. I've told your officers everything I know." She reaches to push her long hair behind her ear. "Whoever it is has a sick sense of humor."

"They certainly have."

"Why would they want to get Emily back here?"

"We believe it has something to do with her daughter."

"Daughter?"

"Yeah, Em has a daughter, Lucy. She's fifteen apparently."

Ali looks clearly confused. "But that would have made Emily…"

"Nineteen when she had her. Lucy is Jake's daughter," I cut in.

"That's the reason she and her family left Sandbroke so suddenly?"

"Yeah, turns out Jake wasn't exactly what you would class as a good role model as a father. Currently in prison up north." I don't elaborate on his crimes; I've already said more than I should.

Ali nods. "I never liked him from the get-go, but there was no telling her back then," she whispers. "Poor Em."

"Look, can you come through? We need to interview you. Emily's daughter could be in danger. We need any further info at all that you have."

"There is something," she says suddenly.

"What's that?"

"It just occurred to me on the way over here. It's probably nothing. I could be totally wrong."

"Wrong about what, Ali?"

"The book. The one you said was found at the beach."

"What about it?"

"Well, I think I got mixed up. All the other stuff that was found in the bag was from the jumble sale, but that book that Chrissy mentioned was the one I had signed by my favourite author. I stood for almost two hours at a bookstore in London waiting to get it signed."

"So, what are you saying?"

"There were other books amongst the things in the jumble sale, but I don't think that one was with them. I would never have given that book away. It meant too much to me."

"So you are saying it was taken?"

Ali bows her head, when she looks back up at me, her brown eyes are filled with worry.

"I think the book must have been taken from the shelf in my bedroom." Her shoulders are trembling, and I resist the overpowering urge to reach out and pull her into a tight embrace and tell her that everything will be alright. That over my dead body would I let anything bad happen to her. Instead, I move my hands to rest lightly on her shoulders.

"Ali, I need you to think, is there any way anyone could have had access to your home?"

"You mean anyone that could have broken into my house?"

"Not necessarily. Is there anyone you let in willingly?"

"That's easy," she replies. "There were only ever two people I had that sort of relationship with since I've been back here, you and my friend that I met at the hospital."

"Your friend you met at the hospital?"

"Yeah, you remember, don't you? I'm sure I would have mentioned her to you. I met her at a hospital volunteer day. We ran the Tombola together at the kids fair in Cranley. I found out she went to the same psychotherapist as me when I lost my mum."

I honestly don't remember her ever mentioning anything when we had been seeing one another. If she did, it must have only been in passing. It obviously hadn't been enough for me to remember.

I rush Ali through to my office and yell at Chrissy to come and join us, whilst trying my best not to look at Ali. I can smell the perfume she is wearing and it brings back memories of the time we spent together. Sweet, like vanilla.

"Chrissy, I think we might have a lead," I yell.

Chrissy jogs from the back of the room and joins me at the office door. She pauses as she sees Ali and gives her a warm smile. Ali returns the gesture, looking a little uncomfortable and now thoroughly confused.

"I think I might have a lead too," says Chrissy. She nods down at a manila folder she holds, then she looks back at Ali, unsure of whether to continue to tell me her discovery in her presence.

"It's okay, go on, Chrissy," I urge.

Chrissy nods, and takes a step further into the office.

"I've found out who the mother of Jake's daughter, Mia was." She passes me an enlarged photo from the file she's grasping. It's from a Yorkshire-based newspaper dated just over a year ago. Before I have a chance to take it, Ali jumps up from her seat and moves to my side, snatching the piece of paper from Chrissy's hand.

"That's her," she announces loudly.

"Who?" asks Chrissy, undoubtedly perplexed.

"That's my friend, the one I've just been talking about." She looks at me, her eyes wide. "Why do you have a photograph of her?"

I take the paper from Ali and inspect it myself. Something about the girl in the picture looks familiar; petite, small black-framed glasses hiding pretty, large, green eyes. Her hair is a different colour in this photo, dyed dark brown, but it's obvious to me almost instantaneously who this woman is. I remember her from back at school and see her around town occasionally now.

"Shit," I say angrily, as my phone starts to ring, I reach into my pocket to answer the call from the police in Newcastle.

"Who is she Mark?" asks Chrissy urgently.

I slam my fist against the desk making both Ali and Chrissy jump. I'm annoyed that I've been so blinded by the situation with Ali; I'd failed to see something I should have picked up on well before now. "It's Rose Donnelly," I reply. "It's been Rose Donnelly all along."

Chapter 36
Rose

The first thing that you need to know about me is that I'm not really a bad person. A little messed up; probably, a little screwed in the head most definitely, but not really what I would categorize as bad. I didn't want it to come to this, it's just the way things worked out. You understand, right Emily?

I would watch you all the time back when we were at school. You were always so confident and positive, talented too. Everything you did, you seemed to excel in. You had so much ahead of you and could have picked any path that you wanted.

Jake was a good man, and yes, he made mistakes, but then haven't we all? He doesn't deserve the future he has been given and will now be in prison until he is an old man. He will be lucky to ever see the light of day again. But who are you to care? You moved on with your life, just like I have tried to do. But I can't.

We started to see each other when you were still together, Jake and I. We met at the building firm he worked for in Cranley, where I was temping at the time. I knew I wasn't the only one, there were a couple of other women in his life and that didn't matter back then. I was glad when you left him and the two of you finally split up for good. However, I also knew you were the one that he would never forget and he hasn't. To this day, I'm sure he still wonders what it would have been like to still be with you. The one that got away.

We had only been together a short time when we moved away from Sandbroke and had a reasonably good life together for a while. We had a child together and I hoped to one day be Jake's wife, but things soon started to get bumpy and he kept getting himself into trouble.

Then, the car crash happened and he was sent down for causing the death of our daughter. He had been riding the wrong path for years by then. He had been in and out of prison for numerous reasons and was a consistently heavy drinker. One day he took it too far, resulting in him killing Mia.

My whole world suddenly came crashing down around me that day. I struggled to cope alone. I moved back to my old home town and for a while I got on with my life. I endeavored to put Jake behind me, and slowly started to succeed. I tried with all my might to get over losing Mia too. I couldn't.

I met Ali at a charity event at the hospital in Cranley soon after I had returned to Sandbroke. She was in a real mess back then, wracked by grief from losing her mother so suddenly. She was seeing a bereavement counselor and so was I, to help me with the loss of my daughter, the same one in fact. What are the chances?

We started talking and soon found we had quite a bit in common. Of course, she didn't know who I was. She didn't remember me from school, as I knew she wouldn't. Soon I began to hatch a plan—to use her to get you back to Sandbroke.

We saw each quite a few times. She kindly let me into her life and her home, as I anticipated she would. Her relationship with Mark Logan hadn't worked out in the way she had hoped. I honestly felt sorry for her. She was heartbroken and I'm ashamed to say I used her state to my advantage. I set everything up to make it appear that Ali had gone missing. I knew she had gone to stay with Jenna for a couple of weeks, so it was a perfect opportunity to get you back to Sandbroke. Everything worked exactly as I planned. Congratulations, Emily, you fell into every trap I set.

I was in the perfect position to make your life hell, which I admit is all I intended to do. Why should you get to live a perfect life after being with Jake, when I couldn't? I was also intrigued to see what the woman Jake had never really gotten over looked like now.

When I discovered you had a daughter and that Jake was her father everything changed. I was shocked that Jake had never found out about her, but I never told him. Instead, I went to find her. Once I did, I had full intentions of telling her all about her dad. I took a picture of her shopping and sent it to you. I got the gun from an old contact of Jake's, the same person who also showed me how to hack into a personal e-mail account. Just one of the many non-law abiding citizens that he is well acquainted with. I took the gun with me, not to harm anybody, but I admit I wanted to scare you.

I pray for your forgiveness one day, Emily. I understand that it's a big ask, but until you have been in my position you will never know how it feels. What more can I say?

See you soon.

Chapter 37

I sit in the kitchen of my home staring at a space in the middle of the table I have polished more than ten times since I returned home an hour ago. It's strange to think that it was only five days ago that this whole thing started. This is the same place I sat when I spoke to Chrissy on the telephone and learnt of Ali's supposed disappearance. Where this story began is also where it will end.

Lucy is now in the hospital getting checked over by the doctors, but I've been assured she is fine. In fact, I think at this moment in time she is handling things better than I am. Mum and Dad have gone with her and left me to have some time alone. Although I declined their offer profusely, they insisted that I would be better off coming home rather than going to the hospital after I had spoken to the police earlier. In the end, I agreed.

I told the police everything I know and I am no closer to justifying the reasons behind what Rose did. I can only imagine it was done through the pain of losing her daughter and the torture that Jake must have put her through. Now Rose is dead, and I won't ever get answers to the questions I have. I hope that one day I will be able to forgive her for what she did.

Right now, though, it seems impossible. They say time is a great healer and I'm hoping that in this case, it is.

Mark called me earlier and filled me in on the final missing puzzle pieces after speaking with Ali further, which has made me see how incredibly simple Rose's whole plan was.

The car that tried to run me over was found stored in a garage at Rose's mum's home where Rose started living when she returned from Yorkshire and took over managing the holiday park a year ago, just after Mia had died. The car was a red mini cooper registered to Rose. Along with the car, during a search of the property, the police also found a black wig and more of Ali's clothes, among them a pale blue shirt. The person I thought I saw and that Claudia thought she saw at the holiday park was never Ali at all, just Rose cleverly disguised to look like her. She'd been playing games as she had been since the start when she sent me the e-mail, toying with us all to get to what she really wanted all along—me.

Rose had taken a spare key from Ali's home on one of the occasions she had been invited in for a coffee and got copies made, one of which she gave to me, before replacing it so Ali was none the wiser. The other, she kept herself, enabling her access into Ali's house whenever she wanted. They will never know if Rose was ever in the house at the same time as Ali without Ali knowing. From all angles it seemed Rose was a chancer, so the possibility is high that this may have happened at some point. She had also stolen personal items some with Ali's handwriting, making it easy for her to forge the notes to me. It's all so clear now. The e-mail was used to get me back to

Sandbroke, and using Ali was an easy way to do this because she knew how close we once were. The notes, messages, and fake sightings of Ali were all to make sure I stayed in Sandbroke. What her eventual plans were for me I'll never know. Her original plans changed the moment she found a photo of Lucy in my purse at the cabin, and discovered Jake had another daughter.

I honestly don't believe that she came here to harm Lucy. I think she couldn't bear the fact that my daughter was alive and hers wasn't. She wanted to see her in the flesh, and when she did, she became jealous of me, which is why she sent the photo and held my daughter at gunpoint, not to harm Lucy, but to put me through pain too. I saw the photo of Mia; her resemblance to Lucy was uncanny. Two beautiful young girls, one of whom was sadly robbed of a future by the one person who should have gone out of his way to protect her. In my eyes, Jake is the one who deserves to be dead.

When Lucy returns from the hospital, she heads straight to bed, exhausted by the day's events. I tuck her in and lightly kiss her on the forehead, something I have done since she was a baby. I continue to clean the house using any excuse to preoccupy my mind.

When Lucy wakes a couple of hours later, we lie on the sofa and watch films. I order a pizza for us and we chat just like we always do. She tells me the truth about her trying to track down Jake and I tell her the truth about where I have really been for the last four days. We swear we won't lie to each other ever again. Things once again start to feel a little more normal and I silently praise my daughter for her undeniable resilience.

Later that night, I show Lucy the photos I took whilst I was in Sandbroke and when one flashes up of Tom taken on the night we went out, I feel my heart flutter. I silently curse myself for leaving him the way that I did, knowing full well I've lost out on the chance of something special. Lucy tells me he's gorgeous and playfully teases me as I flush madly with embarrassment. She asks me to tell her all about him, so I do, right from the start all those years ago. She listens intently as I speak. Mark told me on the phone earlier today that Tom is doing well after he was pushed from the balcony by Rose and is now out of hospital recuperating at home. I am pleased. Tom is a good and decent man, and he will always hold a special place in my heart—which he has never really left.

It starts to get late. Lucy has clearly developed a second wind, but I am exhausted. She pulls a blanket over me as my eyes grow heavy. My body is too weak from tiredness and the stress of today to fight against it.

"I love you," I manage to say through a sleepy haze that beckons me as she kisses me on the forehead just as I had done her a few hours ago.

"I love you too, Mum," she replies, as she switches off the light. I'm asleep by the time she passes me again, with my phone in her hand, already texting Tom Logan's number.

Epilogue

I pull the woolen blanket around my shoulders as a nip in the air presents itself. The fire has started to pick up now, and crackles against the dimming evening light. Night is fast approaching. In the distance, my best friend playfully skips in and out of the water, once again back to the fun-loving and carefree girl I remember so well. Music plays in the distance accompanied by the wonderful sound of laughter as people enjoy themselves on a pretty late summer's evening.

"So, do you think you made the right decision moving back to Sandbroke?" asks Mark, as he passes me a lager from the cool bag resting on the sand at his side. I take a sip, then nod. He doesn't even need to ask. Sandbroke is my home; I was always going to end up back here, somewhere down the line. Destiny had this chapter of my life written for me well before I even knew it existed.

More people continue to join the party, some familiar faces and some new ones that I look forward to getting to know. I smile and wave as I spot Lucy through the crowd, where she stands outside Logan's Tavern laughing. She's joined by the two girls she met when we first arrived here that she now classes as her best friends. She's recently completed her first year of an art course at college. Seems she has a real flare for it, and I've never seen her happier. Her watercolours of Ceaders Bay, which take pride of place on the walls of our new home, are nothing short of phenomenal. She has recently painted one to send as a house warming gift to my parents, who are now living up the coast from us in their beloved village of Pemblington.

Ali races back up the beach where Mark wraps his arms around her and swings her in a full circle before she drops down next to me on the sand. She grabs the corner of my blanket and pulls it around us both. The diamond engagement ring on her left hand catches in the setting sun and Mark winks as she smiles at him through the fire. The ring he once wore on his left hand is now gone.

"Glad you're back, Em," she says, as she rests her head on my shoulder.

"Me too," I reply.

We sit in silence, watching the waves as people continue to dance and laugh around us. Our friendship is stronger than ever, bonded tighter by the time that has passed with the absence of each other in our lives.

"Em, I could do with a hand. Do you mind coming up and helping behind the bar for a bit? We are swamped tonight," Tom whispers into my ear from behind me. His lips brush against my cheek as he crouches down and kisses me lightly, then wraps his arms around my shoulders.

"No problem, boss," I answer. He pulls me to my feet and then turns to make his way back to the bar and the party he is hosting tonight to celebrate its three-year anniversary.

"Slave driver," says Mark, punching his brother on the arm jokingly as he passes.

Tom laughs, ignoring Mark's sarcasm. "You don't mind if I steal her for a bit, do you?" Tom asks Ali. She catches his eye and gives him a bright smile.

"Not at all. Mark and I are heading off now anyway, we have to get back to the boys," says Ali, as she rises to join us. Mark's two sons are as much a part of Ali's heart now as she is his.

I smile and give my friend a tight hug.

"Bye, Ali."

She waves as she and Mark finish saying their goodbyes and make their way along the beach hand-in-hand. "See you later Em," she turns to shout to me, before they disappear into the night. I throw up my hand and wave back. Tom meets me and puts an arm around my waist as we walk in the opposite direction, "Yes, Ali," I shout back to her, "see you soon."

Acknowledgements

I would like to thank everyone who has supported me by purchasing, reading, reviewing and recommending my books so far, and for all the amazing messages and words of encouragement you have kindly taken the time to send. It's nerve wracking putting your work out there for the world to see, particularly within such a hugely competitive industry, but you have made it all so much easier.

A big thank you to Christie for jumping to my rescue, completing the edit in time for my desired publish date and for sharing some brilliant words of wisdom.

Last but never least, thanks once again to my lovely family and friends for supporting me throughout. Here's to book number three!

About the author

NC Marshall was born and raised in the North East of England, where she still lives with her fiancé.

As a keen reader, she has always wanted to write a novel of her own and has held a dream of doing so since she was young.

She enjoys travelling, and likes to get inspiration for her writing from the various places that she has been lucky enough to visit.

NC Marshall's debut novel, 'Sleep Peacefully' is listed as an Amazon UK bestseller in its categories and reached the number 1 best seller chart position in the Paranormal Suspense genre.

Before you go

Enjoy See You Soon? Here is a sneak peek at the prologue of NC Marshall's debut novel, Sleep Peacefully.

Praise for Sleep Peacefully

"Sleep Peacefully is a fantastic novel full of suspense and mystery, with many twists and turns which are sure to keep you guessing. I look forward to reading more from this talented author."
-Fresh Fiction

"This is a phenomenal debut from NC Marshall that had me gripped from start to finish!"
-The Book Magnet

"Without doubt, this is an extremely well-written and cleverly crafted novel that I could not put down and did not want to be parted with in the slightest!"
-Hannah's Book Reviews

"The best book I have read in a very long time. I look forward to the authors next. She has a definite wonderful gift!"
-Amazon customer

"You start with questions, and through Nat's pursuit you pass secrets, lies, dramatic revelations and a wisp of mortal danger. NC Marshall deserves credit for her well thought out and provoking tale."
-Bloghound

Sleep Peacefully

NC Marshall

Sleep Peacefully
Prologue

It's the night that I will always remember as if it were yesterday. I can still recite every moment, running it through my mind like scenes extracted from a well-written play. I can recall every last detail with remarkable clarity. Unfortunately, though, this wasn't a play; there was no set, no cast or props, and I had no understudy to step in and seamlessly take my place if required. This was reality. It was my reality, it was my life, and in less than ten minutes time it was going to change forever.

It was approaching the middle of January, the tenth to be exact. It was the early hours of the morning following the coldest day we had experienced in a while, and had just turned twenty-three minutes past two. I knew this because I hadn't slept a wink. I'd been awake all night, with an awful dose of a winter flu bug that had struck everyone I knew. I'd had it for a number of days, but it wasn't easing in its ferocity and I couldn't seem to shake it. Even though the temperature in the room had dropped drastically since I'd gone to bed a few hours earlier, I lay with the covers thrown back, hot and bothered, growing increasingly more aggravated.

The illuminated digital numbers on the clock next to me gradually increased. I lay watching them slowly roll by, the seconds crawling forward one by one. I counted them silently as they passed, wishing them to move faster so that the daylight would break and the long night would be over.

I wriggled my body, trying to loosen my aching muscles, then shifted from the cramped-up position that I had adopted, moving my legs and spreading them out across the other side of the double bed, which was cold and empty. I was alone that night; my husband had been working away that week, like he often did. It didn't bother me, not anymore, I was now used to sleeping alone. My arm had gone dead from staying in the same position for too long. I removed it from underneath my pillow and wiggled it, resulting in a rush of pins and needles running from my elbow to my fingertips.

I'd pretty much given up on the idea of getting any rest at all that night, and had been contemplating going downstairs to get myself a hot toddy. It was a cold and flu remedy that my dad had always sworn by. The welcome haze of alcohol induced slumber seemed appealing, and I was just about to make a move when my mobile phone rang from somewhere beside me.

I glanced once again at the clock. It was two-thirty a.m. on the dot, and even though I was wide awake, the shrill tone of the phone ringing out into the silence still made me jumpy. I searched around, blind in the darkness, moving my hands in the direction of the sound, and eventually found the phone buried under the bedclothes.

I remember squinting my eyes at the caller display, its brightness making my vision go momentarily blurry. However, my eyesight quickly returned to normal, enabling me to make out the caller's identity; it was Matt, my brother-in-law. Before I even held the phone to my ear, a terrible and gut-wrenching feeling of dread hit me. It was almost as if I'd half-guessed his reason for calling. Of course, there was no way I could have possibly known. I hesitated a few seconds and tried to clear my throat before I finally answered.

"Hello," I whispered, my voice croaky. My throat felt like I'd swallowed a pint of broken glass as I spoke. The line was silent. I was just about to hang up, assuming that Matt had called my mobile by mistake, when I heard the faint sound of breathing coming from the other side of the line.

"Matt, is that you? What's wrong?" I felt myself physically tense up, my whole body freezing from head to toe as I waited for his reply.

"Natalie, something's happened, it's Jess, she..." Matt stopped mid-sentence and paused for a while before he continued. It was obvious something was terribly wrong. His voice barely resembled the one I knew, his words coming out rushed and muddled. I could tell he was in shock. I waited. He was trying to speak while choking back quiet sobs. He wasn't making a lot of sense at first. Then he managed to compose himself a little and said three words that hit me like a forceful blow, three simple words that I won't ever forget.

"Jess is dead."

I remember thinking I'd misheard him at first, surely I had? But then the harshness of reality kicked in, and I knew I hadn't. My left hand shot up to cover my mouth, desperately trying to hold back a scream that threatened to escape from my lips. My right hand lost its grip on the phone and it dropped to the floor. It landed silently on the carpet face down. I could still hear the sound of Matt's muffled, distraught voice coming up from it.

I pinched at my bare arms, digging my nails deep into my skin, desperate to wake myself from the nightmare I had entered. In the dim light, I could see the marks I had created, but I didn't wake up, I *couldn't* wake up. Putting my hands over my ears, I shook my head, trying to block out the sound of Matts's voice. *This can't be happening. I'm dreaming, I must be dreaming. Wake up Nat, for God's sake wake up!*

Reluctantly, I removed my hands from my ears, my already foggy head grew heavier, and the bedroom started to swim around me. Everything felt strangely dreamlike and progressed in slow motion. My lungs were burning and my heart hammered at lightning quick speed. I clenched my chest, trying to inhale more air, I felt as though I couldn't get enough, as though my airways had closed up. *I'm going to stop breathing. Do something!*

After a few moments of frantically trying to catch my breath, I reached down to retrieve the phone. But as I did I knocked over a full jug of water from the bedside cabinet, which was still there from my bedridden day before. It fell to the floor, some spilled out over my bare feet and the remainder settled in a large pool near them. I steadied myself against the bed, blood pounding in my ears and stood up shakily, feeling lightheaded. I tried to move my legs, but my knees buckled and I wobbled backwards. Eventually, I found my balance, rooted my feet to the spot, and bent down to scoop up the phone. Pressing it back to my ear, I prepared myself for what Matt had called to tell me.

Jess had fallen from a cliff top earlier that night. The police had shown up at Matt's apartment shortly after discovering her body on the rocks below. Her handbag and ID hadn't been far from where she had landed, so it had been easy to contact her next of kin.

I think he told me more, he'd gone into detail about what the police believed had happened, but at that point I couldn't take in any further information. My brain had stopped working, it simply couldn't absorb anything else. My little sister was dead.

I can't recall much after that brief conversation with Matt. After I hung up I remember feeling totally numb. I'd slid to the floor, sitting cross-legged on the wet patch of carpet near the bed. Water soaked up through the thin material of my pyjama bottoms, but I remained in the same position, staring at a blank space on the wall of the room, unable to move. My skin felt cold and damp, and my body shook profusely.

The almost full moon outside shone brightly through a gap in the curtains, creating a perfectly straight line of white light, which settled on a chair at the far side of the room. For a brief moment, I even thought I saw her. Jess. She was sitting on the chair, her posture relaxed, with one foot up on the seat tucked under her leg and her head cocked to the side, as if carefully studying my state of despair. A look of concern clouded her delicately featured face. I shook my head and she disappeared.

I sat there in the dark for quite a while before realising that I was going to have to call my mum. Matt had found it hard enough to tell me; he wasn't going to be making any other calls. My hands trembled violently as I tried to find her number on my phone. I was still conscious enough to know that it was my responsibility to alert the rest of my family about Jess's death.

After two botched attempts at making the call I was successful. Mum answered on the third ring, and I took a deep breath to steady my voice before I slowly started to tell her that her youngest daughter was dead. To this day, it's the most difficult thing I've ever had to do.

We soon found out that Jess was drinking heavily that night. She had been going through a few personal problems at the time, and turning to drink to kill the pain wasn't out of character for her. The police had carried out a brief investigation, but nothing suspicious was found. They believed that she had been up on the cliffs alone, probably just walking, which she used to do on a regular basis so it was nothing out of the ordinary. She would have been unsteady on her feet under the influence of alcohol, and had roamed too close to the cliff edge. The surface there was very unstable and she could have easily lost her footing, sending her into a sheer drop to the rocks below.

For over eight months now, I have lived with the pain and persistent torture brought on from losing my sister that night. For all this time, I have had no reason to believe that her death was anything more than a tragic accident... until now.

Thank you so much for reading this book. If you have enjoyed See You Soon, it would be great if you could spare a few minutes to leave a short review on Amazon. Reviews play a major part in a books visibility and overall success.

Also, feel free to connect with NC Marshall online. She would love to hear from you:

Facebook page: https://www.facebook.com/pages/NC-Marshall/687071924758804
Twitter: http:/twitter.com/nc_marshall
e-mail: ncmarshall15@yahoo.co.uk

14285591R00146

Printed in Poland
by Amazon Fulfillment
Poland Sp. z o.o., Wrocław